Faith in Cripple Creek

CRIPPLE CREEK SERIES, BOOK 3

SARA R. TURNQUIST

MOUNTAIN
SUMMIT PRESS

If you would like to stay up-to-date on this and other series from Sara and receive a free ebook, sign up for her newsletter:

https://saraturnquist.com/list

*For Becky,
I hear your rendering of the character
voices in my head when I write.
Thanks for bringing them to life through audio.*

CHAPTER 1

Arrival

This had to be the worst day of her life. Jane Millington opened her eyes. Had the stagecoach stopped? Her teeth still seemed to vibrate despite the lack of forward momentum.

Indeed, her eyes confirmed what her body could not—the shaking heat box on wheels no longer sped through the town.

She looked out the window and coughed. Dust surrounded the vehicle. Still, she peered beyond. The stores, rustic to be sure, lined the main stretch. Did everything have to be covered in dirt? The buildings looked as if a thorough scrub would do them good. But what could she expect from such a provincial town?

Her gaze wandered to the platform. The small cluster of people looking in the direction of the coach did not seem threatening. But where was her friend? She had endured this journey with only that hope intact—that she would see Kitty, her dearest, closest friend at its conclusion.

"Miss?" a rough voice cut through the fog surrounding her thoughts.

The driver stood beneath the door, a worn expression on his face.

For certain, the trip jarred him as much as it had her. Why, then, did he insist on traveling at such speeds?

"We're here," he continued.

As she watched, limbs still frozen in place, he reached for the latch and opened the door.

"Cripple Creek." He spat. Something dark and foul came from his mouth, landing a short distance from him in the dirt.

Jane swallowed and her stomach twisted. Was such a lack of manners common in Cripple Creek?

"You all right, miss?" The driver looked at her again, an eyebrow raised.

How could she tell him about the roiling in her stomach? Which was more to blame—the upset of the coach ride or the small dark wet puddle inches from the man's boot?

"You seem a bit...pale." The driver's features shifted from the stale tired expression to one that mimicked concern.

"I'm..." She wanted to say *quite well*. But her inability to quell her nausea did not help matters. She peeled her fingers loose from the window opening and pressed the back of her hand to her lips. Perhaps that would prevent an unladylike and untimely emptying of her last meal.

"I don't need this," the man declared. He turned away, muttering something about 'females.'

Her face heated. Not a pleasant addition to her unease.

"Sir," the driver called to someone farther away. "I got a lady needs a doctor. You know where I can find one?"

Jane shut her eyes. This wasn't happening.

"Miss?" another, somewhat kinder voice spoke into the confining space.

She only dared open one eye to see who else had come to witness her embarrassment. Oh, why hadn't someone been sent to meet her? Kitty had *promised* that she would be here.

The man that now looked in seemed genuine in his concern. He was taller than the driver. Broader of shoulder. His dark hair grew past his collar, and his unshaven face betrayed the beginnings of a beard. But it was his eyes...his deep brown eyes, mirrors of her own...that caught her. When she met his gaze, she could breathe again.

"May I take you to the town's doctor?" His voice was smooth even as his eyes seemed pained. By what?

"I...I..." This was not the time to lose her words! She sucked in a breath and let it out slowly. "I think I may just need some fresh air." Indeed her uneasiness abated now that the coach had stilled.

The man with the brown eyes turned his head. What did he seek?

No one stood behind him.

The driver had moved off. Where had he gone? Surely, he wouldn't abandon his responsibility.

Her would-be savior shot out a breath. "Typical."

What did that mean?

He turned back to her. "Please, miss, let me help you." Extending his hand into the coach, he waited.

And waited.

His gaze landed on her, a question in his eyes.

Was she staring? She jerked back. And almost toppled off the bench.

Hands gripped her forearms.

As she righted herself, she found she was only inches from the man. Had he stepped into the coach?

She couldn't tear her eyes away from his enough to take in the situation. As she blinked, she became more aware of their precarious positioning. And her cheeks warmed once again.

"Are you sure you don't need to see the doctor?" His eyes darkened. He did seem rather concerned.

"No, sir. I thank you. But I am quite well." Though she asserted it to be so, her voice sounded weak even to her.

He pulled back, stepping out of the coach. But he kept a firm hold on one of her hands. And so, as he removed himself from the space, he brought her as well.

Now in the open, she blinked against the bright sunlight. And allowed him to guide her forward as her eyes adjusted.

She took in her surroundings once again. She had a better view of the rows of buildings lining the main dirt road. It was more than she'd expected of this small town. Still not what she would consider a comfortable place to live by any means. How did one survive with so few businesses to patronize? But it was quaint. Endearing even. Though perhaps impossible to clean.

"Is someone expecting you?"

The man's question drew her attention back to his face. With his mouth drawn into a thin line and his brows furrowed, she wouldn't say he welcomed her interrupting his day.

Pity.

She looked away, chastising herself for thinking such a thing. That wasn't right. It wasn't as if she were free to notice such things.

"Miss?" His head dipped and he squeezed her hand.

Only then did she realize he still held to her fingers. His touch anchored her and sent tingles up her arm. Goodness, she was out of sorts.

"I...did expect my friend to meet me. She must have been delayed."

He frowned as he glanced down the street. As if seeking out some sort of salvation.

How did she get herself into such messes?

Sighing, he released her hand. Did he just now realize he retained his hold? "I can't very well leave you standing out here. Alone."

"That's kind of you, sir. But I can manage until..."

He waved a hand between them. "Let me walk you to the café. At least there you'll be comfortable while you wait."

She swallowed. Should she take him up on his offer? Or dismiss his aid? He appeared rather put off already. But maybe that was just her own embarrassment. There was no reason to think him anything other than a perfect gentleman.

"Thank you," was all she managed.

He nodded. "I suppose it's the least I can do."

As he turned, she wondered after his statement. He had already assisted her rather awkward exit from the coach.

The coach!

She put a hand on his forearm. "My bags—"

He turned only halfway. "The driver will put them by the telegraph office. They'll be safe there."

Uncertain, she glanced at the small building beside the stagecoach where the driver piled bags and trunks.

When she shifted her focus back to her guide, he stared at her hand upon his arm.

She snapped it back as quickly as possible.

His eyes found hers once more. There was something deeper in those hazelnut orbs than she could discern. Something swirling in his thoughts. It entranced her.

"Please," he said as he held out a hand toward the far end of the road. "Shall we continue?"

"Yes." She picked up step beside him.

The silence between them became tense. She so dreaded silence, and the awkwardness that came with it.

"I'm Jane," she spit out.

"Miss?"

"My name—Jane Millington." She allowed herself another glance in his direction.

He was not looking at her. Rather his face turned opposite, peering at something in the distance.

Her introduction and his lack of response did nothing to improve the awkwardness. Perhaps it even made it worse.

He veered to the right and stopped just short of an open door. There were tables and chairs within and the smell of meat and vegetables. As well as cobbler.

Her stomach growled. It had been a while since she'd eaten. But she wasn't certain if the gentleman would join her. Or was this where they parted?

Turning back to him, she pressed a smile to her lips. "I thank you...for your assistance."

He continued to watch the café. Was there something of great interest within? If so, she could not discern it.

Tightening her smile, she nodded and stepped over the threshold and into the café.

"Timothy."

She spun. "Pardon?"

"My name is Timothy. Perhaps I'll see you around town."

Her mouth moved, but no words came forth. And in the next instant, he had walked away.

She would have to ask about this Timothy. What, if anything, did her dear friend Katherine Matthews Sullivan know of him?

Timothy resisted the urge to turn back toward the intruding woman. He would not. Instead, he focused on the ground in front of his feet as they carried him farther and farther away.

Lost. Helpless. Infernal woman.

Why did he think it was his job to help her? It wasn't as if it were his fault she'd been alone. Who had left her so hapless at the station?

It didn't matter. He couldn't afford her any more thought. Not one more thought for her brown hair that shimmered with golden strands when she'd stepped out of the stagecoach. Or how the light had highlighted a sprinkle of freckles across her nose.

He shook his head. *No!*

He must take his thoughts captive. These musings would not take him anywhere pleasant. It couldn't.

By now, he noted that his strides had taken him beyond the town center. He found himself moving through tall grasses closer to the schoolhouse.

He halted, hands fisted at his hips. Dropping his head back, he closed his eyes and let out a breath. *Why must you tempt me?*

Nothing.

Have I not paid my dues?

He snorted. Why would he expect anything? There was no answer to be had.

Rustling nearby caught his attention. He jerked his regard in the direction of the sound.

A tall, aged oak stood several feet away. Within its shade, behind its trunk, there was movement.

What was that? Or who?

Three young boys ran out from behind the massive tree. The first clung tightly to something in his grasp. And the others laughed as they followed.

Narrowing his gaze, Timothy attempted to home in and determine what had so enraptured them. He did not like the look of it.

The boys didn't pay any mind that they rushed in his direction.

Timothy moved to the side and intercepted the leader, hooking the boy with an arm across his chest. "Whoa, there."

Blue eyes stared up at him. The lad gripped his prize even more firmly. "What gives, mister?"

Timothy hardened the muscles in his face at the disrespectful display. Ignoring that, however, he pointed at the boy's hand. "What do you have?"

The boy pulled the arm behind his back. "Nothin'."

Glaring at the other boys, lest they become a threat, Timothy was pleased when they stepped back. Followers only.

"Let me see what you have." Timothy insisted, his own grip shifting to the boy's shoulders. He kept his hold firm, but not incredibly so.

"You're not my pa," the youngster sneered, rising on his toes, and pressing up until he was just short of Timothy's face.

"If you would like, I could escort you home and we could have this conversation with your pa." Timothy kept his tone even, emotionless.

The boy's eyes widened. Was he so fearful of his father?

Timothy's chest ached. Why should a boy be afraid of his own pa? But he knew. And he pitied the lad for it.

"Here." The boy's demeanor changed. He was no longer the aggressive mean kid, but rather a child. Compliant and scared.

The smaller hand came from around his back.

Timothy loosened his grip.

The boy's hands came together and turned slightly. Then he exposed the tiny creature captive in his clutches—a small brown lizard.

Timothy examined the innocent animal. Its breathing was rapid. What else should he expect? It might very well die from having its heart work so hard. But there was a chance it may not.

The boy's eyes were fixed on the reptile.

"Why did you take it from its home?" Timothy knelt, his eyes softening as they met the boy's gaze again.

But the youngster looked down. This time the child shrugged. He was quite near tears, seemingly uncaring of his friends staring at him.

Timothy placed hands under the boy's, still outstretched. "We need to put it back in its home. Where his little lizard family is."

The boy's head bobbed, but he still would not look at Timothy.

Licking his lips, Timothy tried again. "Do you like these? Lizards and snakes and whatnot?"

The big blue eyes met Timothy's again. A jerk of his head was all the boy managed.

Timothy offered a smile. "Me, too." He glanced in the direction of the other boys, hoping to include them. "When I was your age, I used to go on reptile hunts."

That sparked interest. The three sets of eyes were on him.

"And I think," he gently removed the weakened lizard from the boy's still open hands, "that I feel up for a hunt. Maybe later this week?"

The boys exchanged wide-eyed glances.

Timothy stood. "Oh? Would you three like to come?" He pointed between the boys.

They nodded.

He smiled. "Let's check with your parents."

If possible, the boys' eyes became wider. Except the one who'd had the lizard. His head dropped. Because he feared his pa wouldn't let him go? Or because he was afraid to ask?

Timothy put a hand to his shoulder. "Let's get this lizard back and make sure you get home."

A chorus of "yes, sir" followed and they moved off to the tree they had just left behind. How far had they carried the little animal? How likely was it to survive? Timothy didn't know. But he was thankful he now had a place for his thoughts that did not involve the hapless woman from this morning.

Jane shoved a spoonful of vegetable beef stew into her mouth. The savory meat filled her stomach, but did little to distract her.

Where was Kitty? Had something happened?

And why had that man, Timothy...something, seemed so put off?

No. That last thought was probably out of place. Dear Lord, she had barely set foot in Cripple Creek and here she was, fawning over the first man she met...quite literally the first one.

What was wrong with her? Was she so desperate?

At that moment a breathless woman rushed into the café.

"Ms. Abby, have you seen—" she started, before halting and gasping for more air.

Jane turned in that direction. *Katherine!*

Jerking upright, Jane nearly toppled her glass of water. "Kitty?"

"Oh, Jane!" Katherine put a hand to her heart. Her chest heaved. "I have searched everywhere."

Jane moved to intercept her dear friend as Katherine stumbled forward, and they embraced. It was sorely needed. She hadn't realized she'd felt so lost and lonely...for so long.

When Jane pulled back, she drew her brows together. "I had expected you at the station. Did something delay you? Is everything all right?"

"Yes," Katherine managed as she held onto Jane's forearm. "Ellie Mae is with Wyatt. We had some...challenges...at home this morning."

"Challenges?" What could she mean? Was someone injured?

Katherine smiled despite her difficulty regaining her composure. "You'll understand when you have little ones toddling about."

A dagger. Right into Jane's heart.

Her own family. Would it ever happen? Especially now that...

"We should sit and let you finish your meal." Katherine glanced over Jane's shoulder to the recently vacated seat.

Jane looked back at the bowl. She no longer had any appetite. She shook her head and opened her mouth.

"I insist." Katherine tilted her head. "I've interrupted your meal. No doubt one much needed after your travels."

"But I—"

"I won't hear it," Katherine said firmly. "Go, finish your lunch. I need to find Wyatt and tell him to call off the search anyway."

Jane swallowed. How many people were combing this town looking for her?

Katherine smiled and leaned forward, pulling Jane into her embrace again. "I am so glad you have come."

Allowing that contact to provide what comfort it could, Jane was tempted to linger there. But she dare not prolong it. And so, when Katherine pulled back, Jane released her.

"Just give me ten minutes." Jane winked.

"Don't be choking on your food now."

Jane felt the corners of her mouth rise a bit. "I won't."

And then Katherine was gone. Out the door and around the corner. Jane was alone...again.

If possible, she felt even more alone than before.

When you have your own family...

Katherine surely hadn't meant anything by it. Still, it had stung. Deeply.

Jane stepped back to the seat she had occupied moments before and settled into it.

Your own family...

Her eyes pricked. She blinked as she glanced around the room. Everyone seemed intent on their own meals and conversations. Rubbing her arms against a chill that did not exist, she felt exposed, vulnerable.

But she would not let this get the better of her. She would be strong. She *had* to be strong.

That was the way of it.

CHAPTER 2

Opportunity

Timothy crept into the old house, trying in vain to keep the door from creaking. No matter how he oiled the ancient door, the hinges seemed to cry out and announce his presence regardless.

"That you, Timothy?" a voice called from the bedroom attached to the great room.

Mother.

Would she come out?

"Yes. Sorry I woke you."

Rustling of cloth gave him pause. She did intend to free herself from the sheets and approach.

"Please, don't trouble yourself." He made his second vain attempt of the evening. "I can tend to myself."

She grunted.

Timothy moved in the direction of her room but stopped himself after only a couple of steps. She would not welcome his assistance any more than he wished for hers.

She was stubborn. And refused to allow age to take her independence.

Perhaps this was a reflection. A foretelling of his days to come?

Feet padded across the floor.

Though spring had come, the evening still bore a chill. Why must Mother insist on removing herself from the warm comfort of her bed to wait on him? He wanted none of it. But that mattered not to her. It was more for her than him.

She appeared in the dimly lit doorway. Her movements were stiff and slow.

What was it Wyatt had called it? Arth-rit-us? It made it difficult for her to move. To midwife anymore.

Still, Doc had called on her skills when Katherine delivered... when she'd had...

What was the use in revisiting those imaginings? It was no more than a story to him. Told by many. How his mother had stepped in and saved Wyatt and Katherine's child.

And Katie.

Timothy's throat burned. He swallowed against it. The sensation did not lessen.

He looked away from his approaching mother. No need for her to see.

But she would. He could never hide anything from her.

He drew in a cleansing breath. Though the musty smell of the interior of the worn cabin did little to freshen his lungs, it grounded him all the same.

Turning toward his mother's progress, he found her staring at him. Her nearly clear blue eyes boring into him. Spearing him, laying him bare.

"Why are you looking at me like that?" His mother planned, then, to delve into it.

"Like what?" He wiped his features of any emotion, or so he believed.

She quirked a brow. How did she always know when he was lost in thoughts of...what had been and what never would be?

He reached for her arm. "Ma, you shouldn't be up. I can find food for—"

"Don't, Timothy."

He drew his hand back. Her words found their mark.

"She's not yours."

As much as he wanted to look away, walk away, anything...he could not tear his gaze away from hers.

"Never was."

He opened his mouth to argue. But shut it. Too many times they had been down this road. And too many times they had gone in circles. "I'm going to bed."

"What about dinner?" she called after him as he moved past her.

"I'm not hungry," he grumbled.

"She's not the last."

Timothy whirled around. "What?"

Mother faced the window, her eyes no longer on him. "She isn't the only woman. There will be another."

He shook his head. "I...I can't." Keeping his feet planted several paces from her, he looked to the floor. "It's too much. I've lost too much already."

"Hmmm," she murmured.

Leaning slightly toward her, Timothy almost moved in that direction. But he hesitated. He would not be pulled. By her.

Or by another woman seeking only to marry the most eligible man she could find. And that seemed to be what women wanted. He loved his mother, but had she not used her feminine wiles to attract Pa? Manipulate?

He would have none of it.

Turning, he plunged himself into the darker recesses of the house and toward the solace promised in the privacy of his room.

Jane pulled herself out of bed. That had been one of the more difficult nights of her life. Ellie Mae had wakened no less than five times. Screaming.

How did Katherine function? She had not seemed this exhausted yesterday. Was she? Was this a regular occurrence?

Perhaps this had been a bad night for the small child.

Jane stretched. And was surprised when nothing popped. The bed had been comfortable enough, but she had still tossed and turned plenty.

Rising onto the edge of the bed, she slid her legs over the side. The floor was as ice. Jane jerked her feet up. Where was the rug?

She spotted it a couple of inches away. There was nothing else to do but brave the chilled surface. So, she sucked in a breath and pressed her soles to the floor. Padding quickly to the rug, she let out the pent-up air upon settling on the only slightly warmer cloth.

How was she to manage the rest of the morning if she could hardly stand the frigid wood? She closed her eyes and prayed for strength. Was she so far removed from minor inconveniences? It wasn't as if she lived a life of ultimate comfort. She had faced hardships...perhaps too many.

Still, her aunt had made sure she was fed and clothed. A kindness to be sure. For that, Jane should be grateful. And not put so much stock in the kind consideration she saw in Katherine for her children. Or the way Wyatt looked at his wife. Yes, Jane wanted these things. So badly. Would they ever be? She had reason to doubt.

Jane went through the motions of dressing for the day and pulling her hair back. But she noted that her movements were stilted and troubled by the cold air about her.

Though, when she slipped out of the room and into the great room, the fire offered the warmth she craved. Had she not known or suspected that it would be so much cooler in this region? How had she not? Though it wasn't as if she had planned much in advance. Taken hold of an opportunity is more what happened. This was, after all, a chance to get away. To think. To consider...all her options...though limited they may be.

"Good morning." The masculine voice startled Jane, and she whirled around.

Wyatt Sullivan stood over the stove, warming a pot of something. His eyebrows quirked as she watched. "Are you all right?"

Jane calmed her breathing and smoothed down her skirt. "No...I mean yes. That is...I didn't realize you were there."

Wyatt's expression cracked and a half smile slid onto his features. "It certainly wasn't my intention to startle you."

She nodded. And didn't know what to do with her hands. So, she latched them at hip level.

"Would you like some coffee?" His offer was sound and appealed.

"Thank you." She stepped toward the dining table. "Anything I can do to help?"

He shook his head as he moved across the kitchen space and grabbed two mugs.

Jane scanned the room. They were the only two about. Should that make her nervous? Why would it?

Wyatt filled the mugs and brought them to the table, setting one across from the other. At least there would be decent space between them.

She chastised herself. This was a product of her limited knowledge of him. He had not been untoward in any way. And it was clear he loved Kitty dearly. So, Jane pulled out the chair and sat. The warm brew called to her so she sipped some.

And nearly spit it out. The stuff was strong indeed. But she managed to swallow it all the same.

Wyatt's eyes widened. "My apologies. I should have warned you. Seems I like it this way more and more since the baby came."

She allowed a smile to grace her features even as she wrapped her hands around the mug, wishing the heat could fill her being. But dare she drink more? "That's quite all right. I...did notice that Ellie Mae wakes a bit."

Wyatt's brows furrowed. "I hope it didn't disturb you too much."

Jane waved him off. "It was fine," she lied. "Does she do that every night?"

Wyatt nodded and took in another swig of coffee.

"Every night?" That was difficult to imagine. She understood that infants needed to nurse throughout the night, but how did one maintain their sanity on such little sleep?

"Yes, indeed." He watched his mug, a wistfulness in his eyes. Memories of being well rested, no doubt.

"How long will she be that way?" How long would Kitty be without respite?

"It can be weeks...or months. Maybe even a year." Wyatt's words were straightforward and devoid of emotion.

"A year?" she gasped. "I had no idea."

Wyatt nodded and sipped his coffee again.

"And Kitty—Katherine...how is she?"

He shrugged. "It is difficult. She will have the other two during the day as well. I do try to let her get some extra sleep in the mornings, but it's not always possible with the clinic."

Jane frowned. What must her friend be going through? Little sleep, mothering the others as well...was this what it was like for all mothers? Though perhaps it should, it did not dull the ache within Jane for such.

"I...am glad you are here." Wyatt started, but paused. "Katie is thrilled. And I am glad to see that spark in her again."

Jane considered his words. *See that spark in her again.* What did he mean? But as Jane thought on it, she remembered how lackluster Kitty had seemed. And how last night she so often leaned on the counter or against her husband. She was tired. Was that all?

Still, Jane could not bring herself to ask Wyatt these things. For he may well be burdened enough already.

Jane lifted the mug to her lips and took another sip, eager for the added warmth and the effects of the coffee on waking her brain.

And clasped her hand over her mouth as the liquid hit her tongue again.

Wyatt watched her, not even trying to staunch the smile that tugged.

She forced herself to swallow. "I suppose it's something I'll have to get used to."

He nodded and drank some more himself, draining the remainder of his cup. "Here's to that."

Jane allowed her amusement to spread her lips into a smile. But something within still weighed on her. How was her friend? How dire was her situation? And what might Jane do to help? If she even could.

Timothy meandered through the crowd of well-wishers. So much enjoyment. So much merriment. Nothing brought out the lighter side of the townsfolk more than a wedding. But he had done his duty —making an appearance. Why did he feel the need to linger?

His mother's presence was expected by those of her acquaintance. But did anyone truly care if he tarried?

Surely not. He watched the townspeople mill about from his position, settled on the outskirts of the celebrating crowd. He frowned. The happy couple caught his attention. And his chest tightened.

Did they know what lay ahead? The troubles and trials they would face? Then again, he wasn't in a position to judge such things.

While he had counseled a number of married men and women in his time behind the pulpit, he hadn't truly known more than what Scripture spoke of. His advice, then, had only gone as far as his training in such matters. Simply conjecture.

Did he even know what love was?

A deep ache within him acknowledged that he did. He had loved Katherine.

But she was lost to him. And belonged to another.

The adage haunted him for the millionth time: *it is better to have loved and lost than never to have loved at all.* Rubbish. Who needed this hurt?

Tearing his gaze from the dancing newlyweds, whose joy was shared by nearly all present...nearly, he tried to seek out his mother. Perhaps it would be best if he just went home. It was too hard. Besides, no one needed him dampening the joy of the occasion. It wasn't as if he would be missed.

There, by the food table. Mother chattered away with a woman with gray streaked hair. He couldn't place her name, but it mattered not. It wasn't as if he were responsible to know everyone in town. Not anymore.

He rose, destination firmly set in mind. And, taking the few steps his long stride required, he came alongside his mother.

But she was too much involved in the conversation to even notice him. Dare he interrupt? Instinct bade him wait. Injecting himself in the conversation would only bring about a glower from her and a thorough scolding. Some things never changed, no matter how old he might be.

He lingered, waiting for an opening. But as the seconds ticked into minutes, none materialized. The two women lowered their voices and moved to a nearby bench. Had Mother truly not known he was there?

Releasing a breath, Timothy fought to unravel the knot that had formed in his midsection. Why must he endure more of this? Did his mother keep him here on purpose? She must know how all of this affected him. Was she not more mindful?

A young woman with a small child excused herself to pass by him and gather food items for herself and her youngster.

He stepped back from the table, pardoning himself. His gaze swept the assortment of foodstuffs. But he doubted he could stomach anything.

The brightly colored punch, however, seemed like a fine idea.

Side-stepping the woman and child, he made his way to the liquid refreshment.

Two others filled their cups and he waited more patiently than he would have imagined possible. The gentleman in front of him finished and it was Timothy's turn. At last.

But as he reached for the ladle, his hand connected with another. Why couldn't the good people of this town take turns? He had waited, why couldn't they?

He looked up, seeking the identity of this usurper, his mouth tight.

The dark-haired woman from the stagecoach. What was her name? Julia? Jane, perhaps?

"My apologies." Her voice cut through the air a touch louder than necessary as she drew her hand back. "I just..."

Her words trailed as her eyes met his. Did she recognize him? How could she not?

Silence befell them for a few seconds.

That made the moment awkward. As if there were more here between them than there actually was. Still, the ire in him melted. Was it her soft eyes? Or her apology?

"Pardon me, miss." Timothy broke into the stillness, tilting his head forward. "Allow me." He reached for the handle once more and, filling the ladle, he lifted it from the small pool. And waited.

The woman stared at him. What had her so transfixed? Or did she not understand his words?

Timothy furrowed his brows. "Would you like some punch?"

She nodded. "Oh yes, thank you." Thrusting her cup forward, she nearly knocked into the scoop of the ladle.

Timothy couldn't help the smile teasing the corners of his mouth. To say she was flustered would be quite the understatement. She fidgeted all over it seemed—twisting the fabric at her waist, shifting her weight, and glancing about.

He filled her cup and then his own.

Bringing her other hand around to support the now heavier cup, she sipped.

He tried to look away but found he couldn't. She seemed quite unable to gather herself. The way she licked at her lips as if to speak, only to frown and take another sip...it was rather endearing. What had overtaken her?

Part of him wanted to walk away as planned, but he was amused. And curious. Perhaps too much for his own good.

"Are you here with your...*friend*?" He emphasized the last word, letting one side of his mouth lift.

Her eyes widened. She caught his jest. But her flat expression didn't look as if she thought it was funny. Why had he baited her?

"Yes," she pressed out.

"And she is...?" He looked about the immediate area. Would he not just let it go? Why would he lengthen their interaction?

The woman—who he was now certain to be called 'Jane'—put a hand to her face as her cheeks colored.

"She is...attending to something this moment." Jane struggled to get the words out.

"Ah." Timothy raised an eyebrow and took a sip, letting his insinuation be what it was.

Why was he enjoying this? Was he...teasing her? That didn't seem right. Yet he couldn't deny it. He found that the way a pink hue on her cheeks highlighted her features, giving her almost a glow, was alluring.

"But she'll be back." The insistence in Jane's tone told that he'd hit his mark.

"I see." Timothy let his gaze wander over the crowd of dancing merrymakers.

Jane came around to his side of the refreshment table. "I don't think I like your implication, sir." Several inches shorter than he, she stared up into his face. "Kitty is a dear friend and would never—"

Timothy held up a hand. "All right."

Jane's brows arched. "What?"

"I believe you." Timothy set his cup down and took a breath. "I think we may have started off on the wrong foot the other day. And I apologize."

Jane looked off in the opposite direction. Had he surprised her yet again? He liked being one step ahead of her.

But that shouldn't be. What was it about this woman that held such intrigue?

"Shall we?" The words surprised even him as they slipped out. As did his hand, rising in her direction.

"What?" The twist of her eyebrows and pertness of her lips drew him in even more.

"Care to dance?" He shifted his hand closer.

She looked between it and his face.

It seemed as if she wanted to refuse. But in a turn that surprised *him*, she set her cup down and slid a hand into his.

CHAPTER 3

Discovery

J ane kept her eyes on Timothy as he moved her toward the dancing figures. Then he tugged at her, turning her toward himself. As their bodies drew closer, her breath caught. How could that simple action pull at her so? Though it did. The press of his hand on hers brought a warmth with it that she could not ascribe to the sun's heat upon them.

His eyes caught hers expectantly. What did he want?

He held out his other hand. Oh yes, they were to dance. Had she so forgotten herself?

Turning her face so he might not see her blush, she slid a hand up to his shoulder as he placed his at the small of her back. Then they were moving in time with the music.

Jane had not had the occasion to dance often. But she much enjoyed the pastime when she had the chance. It took some effort to force her feet into rhythm with his as they made a waltz pattern.

But he was a good leader. Of that, she was well aware. He moved his own form with grace, easing her along with the cadence of the melody.

She peered up to find his warm eyes on hers. But it was not the intensity she'd expected. There was levity there. Accompanied by a grin, there were small crinkles in the skin beside his eyes. It was the first time, in the limited time she had been of his acquaintance, that he seemed truly pleased with the world.

Her own lips lifted at the corners.

"You dance well, Miss Millington."

"I thank you." Her cheeks warmed at his compliment. "But I fear I would not find my steps so easily were it not for your capable manner."

He smirked at that. "I doubt that very much."

She couldn't find words as his gaze latched onto hers again. This time, there was a depth in the brown orbs that drew her in.

What would it be like to be sought by such a man? Someone who was dark and mysterious, yet had a kind heart. The kind that would help a misplaced woman upon her arrival to a new city?

She caught herself. What was she thinking? It wasn't as if she were free to entertain such thoughts. Or was she? Franklin had made his position very clear. He needed space. And time. Their connection was nothing permanent or binding.

Still, was it right that she cozy up to the first man who showed the least bit of attention? What did that say about her?

"Something amiss?" His tone, laced with genuine concern, crowded out her thoughts.

She shook her head, not willing to give voice to those things churning within. So she allowed herself to enjoy the music and these few minutes of peace. For there were many things to weigh her down. But not in this moment.

Timothy's smile faltered. Had her reaction bothered him so? Or something else?

His attention had fallen elsewhere for a moment. But then, just as quickly, he returned his focus to her face and picked up step once more. Perhaps a bit too forcefully and a touch too fast. And there was a distance about him that had little to do with proper positioning of their bodies, and everything to do with a disturbance of some sort.

She bit her lip to keep from asking after it. That would not be appropriate. He was nothing more than an acquaintance. She dared not push those boundaries. No matter how her heart fluttered.

Timothy's steps slowed, and he came to a halt.

It jarred. Until Jane realized the music had slowed.

He offered her a slight bow.

She responded in kind, with a simple dip of her body.

Then his smile returned. "Thank you for the pleasure of the dance."

He was going to pull away. And all of a sudden, she was frantic to prevent that. Something in his affect tugged at her heart to hold his attention for even a little bit longer.

"Yes. Thank you. It has been quite some time since I had such a fine dance partner." What had she just said? Her cheeks heated. "I meant...capable. Such a capable dance partner."

He looked to the ground, but his mouth widened a bit. At least she had amused.

"I...would very much like that punch now." She attempted to distract him from whatever had fallen so heavily on his shoulders.

He glanced toward the refreshment table and back to her as if weighing his options. A few seconds later he nodded, as if decided, and offered her his arm.

She set a hand in the crook of his elbow and let him lead her once more. This time to the punch bowl.

Pouring each of them a cup, he then drank, but his features had slackened, and the tightness about his eyes had little to do with a smile, rather it appeared as if he were deep in thought. Unpleasantly so.

Dare she try to make light of the moment? She sipped her own punch and wondered how she might go about this. Or should she excuse herself and rejoin Kitty?

Silence fell between them...a silence that threatened to swallow whatever pleasantness had existed. And, for whatever reason, she couldn't allow it.

"Do you have much occasion to dance?" She realized she didn't know his surname. How would she address him?

He shook his head. That was all.

Her whole being drooped. She was useless.

"I hoped you might allow me to thank you again...for assisting me the other day."

He nodded, but his gaze met hers once more in a look that radiated pain.

"You..." she started, hoping to come up with some other distracting question, but relented. "You seem distracted."

There was an intensity in his eyes then and a sadness about his features. "I apologize, Miss Millington. I think I am worn from the long day."

She didn't believe that was all, but she dared not push deeper. It wasn't as if she truly knew this man. Glancing about as she took another swallow of punch, she spotted Kitty not far away. "Oh, there is my friend. I would very much like to introduce you two. Though you probably already know each other. But I know she would like to thank you for coming to my aid."

He grunted but remained as he was.

Jane raised an arm and called out, "Katherine!"

Timothy's hand gripped at Jane's arm. "Your friend is Katherine Sullivan?"

Timothy looked for any avenue of escape around himself. He had to get out of there. He couldn't face Katherine. It was out of the question.

He saw an opening in the crowd to the right and took a step in that direction.

Jane grabbed his arm.

He spun toward her again.

Her wide eyes seemed to plead with him. "She'll just be a minute.

I am so eager to introduce you two. That is, if you don't already know each other." But the emotion behind her gaze was of amusement. She had no inkling, then, of his distress or of his connection to Katherine.

The urge to jerk free and flee pulled at him. It was almost overpowering. But her deep eyes held him to the spot. Why should they?

He shook his head. Enough of this. There was no way he should let himself become ensnared again. Not like this.

Tugging his arm from her grasp, he shook his head. "I...have to be going."

Jane's eyebrows arched as confusion swiped across her features. "I don't understand."

Of course she didn't. How could she? But there was nothing of value for him here. He should just leave. Still, he found himself wanting to explain.

This was wasting precious seconds!

"I just...have to leave." His gaze darted about. Where had Katherine gone? Was she not making her way over here?

"Timothy..." Jane stopped herself.

He balked all the same at her use of his name. Why should that produce the sort of pleasantness that emitted from his core? It couldn't be tolerated.

"I'm sorry. I just...have to go."

She clicked her tongue. That could only signal disappointment.

He would not be moved, however. Stretching out his legs, he turned once more.

And nearly rammed into the very woman he hoped to avoid—Katherine.

Katie's eyes widened as their gazes locked. "Timothy, I..."

What was she going to say? Would he be able to stomach it?

He dropped his regard to the ground. "I, ah, didn't realize..." But he couldn't finish the sentence. Had her very presence rendered him unable to think? It was for this reason he had made every effort to not encounter her since his return.

Jane stepped around him. "Kitty, this is the man I mentioned. The one who helped me the other day."

Her words evaporated and the thick awkwardness enveloped her too.

"Do you two...know each other?" The lightness to her tone just earlier had also vanished. Her words sounded heavier. As if she suspected...or knew.

"I...have to go," he repeated. Then made a move to do just that.

A hand fell on his forearm again, but this touch was more familiar. He peered down at fingers that bore a wedding ring.

"Timothy," Katherine's voice was low, almost sad.

He froze. His name did not belong on her lips. Not now, not ever again. Why did it still affect him so?

"I...had heard you were back in town." She managed to force the words out. It was evident she, too, searched for the ability to endure this exchange.

Jane's breath caught. But Timothy could not make himself care enough to turn and look at her.

Katherine spoke again. "I didn't want to—"

"No." He pulled his arm away and swallowed. "I mean, there is no need to do this." Why couldn't he turn away? Look anywhere else but at her. As if he were drawn in by the radiance of her beauty.

The crowd around them disappeared, and his vision wavered. There was still too much hurt, too much emotion. How would he ever be free?

He did the only thing he could think of—move past her, trying to not let on that the brush of their shoulders seared him. But soon enough, he left the melee behind. And trudged on to...where? It didn't matter. He just needed to go, to run, to breathe.

There was no chance he could weather another heartache. How could he ever let the tiniest bit of hope slip in? And that's what he had done. Let a beam of light in.

He would not make that mistake again.

Best to put Katherine—and Jane—in the past. And leave them there.

"What was that about?" Jane watched Timothy's back as he moved off. His actions were rude, to be sure, but that wasn't what bothered her so. It was his affect...and the pain naked on his expression. Not only did Kitty and Timothy know each other, there was history. The kind that cut deep.

Kitty turned to face her friend. "I'm sorry, Jane."

"For what?" Though Jane's confusion started to clear, there was much she didn't understand.

Kitty sighed—a deep, cleansing exhale. And her gaze moved to the retreating figure, now almost indistinguishable as the merry-makers closed in around them.

"Do you intend to tell me what that was about?" Jane kept her words soft, hoping that her concern was evident to her friend. She didn't want to pry, but she needed to understand, wanted to understand.

Kitty wiped at her cheek. Was she...crying? "Not here."

That wasn't really an answer.

Wyatt appeared, Ellie Mae in his arms, and Susie gripping his pant leg. "I think these girls have had about all they can handle."

Kitty didn't respond. Didn't even turn in his direction.

Wyatt looked between Jane and his wife. "Everything all right?" The curiosity was overshadowed by an edge of concern.

Kitty remained silent, now staring at the ground, her fingers working over the waist of her skirt.

"I think it has something to do with Timothy. He was just here."

Wyatt's gaze darkened. "Katie, you okay? Did he say something to upset you?"

Kitty shook her head.

Wyatt frowned, the skin around his mouth strained. He freed a hand and set it to Kitty's back. "Let me get you home."

Kitty nodded sharply.

He seemed to remember Jane still stood nearby. "I can come back later and collect you if you'd like to stay a bit longer."

"No need," Jane said as she brought a shaky hand to tuck an errant hair behind her ear. Was she trembling? "I'm ready."

Wyatt afforded her a nod but then turned his full attention to his wife, wrapping an arm around her, and drawing her toward the edge of the crowd.

"I don't wanna go, Pa. I'm not tired," Susie said, her voice a whine even as she rubbed at her eyes.

Wyatt did what he could to keep her with him as he maneuvered Kitty and gently bounced Ellie Mae.

Jane reached for the small girl's hand. "Maybe we can play a game when we get home. You enjoy games, don't you?"

Susie nodded and gripped Jane's fingers. A smile crept onto her features.

Wyatt threw Jane a grateful smile before focusing once more on Kitty.

"Why don't we find your brother?" Jane asked Susie as they reached the outskirts of the visiting townsfolk. "Where do you think he is?"

Wyatt and Kitty continued to move on toward the livery.

Jane turned back to Susie.

The little girl scanned the crowd. Perhaps she meant well, but there was little chance from her vantage point she saw much more than skirts and legs.

Jane scrutinized the area. And, some moments later, felt a tug on her skirt.

She looked down and Susie pointed in the direction of the refreshment table. "There he is."

Count one for the girl. Jane had judged her too quickly.

"Let's go—"

"Jack!" the girl yelled, at a higher pitch than Jane was comfortable with. "We gotta go!"

Several heads turned, including Jack's.

His face colored and Jane only then realized he had been speaking with a young girl. Jane would have smiled at that if it weren't for his embarrassment.

He said something to the girl with the golden ringlets and slouching, turned and moved toward their position.

As he neared, Susie reached out her other hand for his.

He enfolded her smaller hand and offered Jane a half smile.

"Your Pa took your Ma to collect the wagon. Your mother... wasn't feeling well."

Jack frowned but didn't ask.

And that felt a little odd to Jane. Was Kitty often not herself? He behaved as if it were a common occurrence. That couldn't be because of Timothy though. It seemed this was the first time they had crossed paths in months. Since...Timothy's return to Cripple Creek? Isn't that what she had said? Why had he left? And what had brought him back?

So many unanswered questions. But they would have to wait. She needed to get these children to their parents and safely home. Then she intended to have a talk with Kitty.

CHAPTER 4

Trouble

Timothy gathered a few tools from the back of his wagon and moved toward the General Store. He nodded and muttered greetings to the few people he passed. Did any of them know of his awkward escape from the wedding? What could he say if anyone brought it up?

So he kept his head down and his interactions brief. After all, it wasn't as if he had the time to spare. He had a job to do.

As he entered the large store, he paused by the counter, waiting while Mr. Yerby finished his conversation with Mrs. Abby. Timothy was loathed to be here...utilizing the carpentry skills his father taught him. Well, repairs really. But he had to do something to occupy his time and bring in much needed funds for his mother and himself. When his father had tried to teach him, he'd been certain he would never use it...except in his own home. Perhaps build a crib, add on a room...

He rubbed at his palm as he watched the store owner converse with the café cook. Calluses had long since formed on his once tender skin. Years of working on sermons and orating from the pulpit had left him soft. In more ways than one.

"Timothy," Mr. Yerby called out, just then seeming to notice.

Mrs. Abby turned in his direction, offering him a pitied smile.

Timothy hated that the most. Why must the townspeople comment on his life...even if it was just with their expressions? It wasn't as if he didn't know how they felt. But did it have to be tossed his way?

He ignored Mrs. Abby's well-meaning look and focused on the reason he was here. "What did you need my help with?"

"Oh, yes!" Mr. Yerby excused himself from his conversation and walked around the counter. "This way."

He led Timothy farther back in the store. There he indicated a collapsed shelf. "I hate to bother you. A couple years ago, I could have managed this myself. But I'm afraid with the arthritis, I'm just not as capable as I was."

The statement did not come with regret or sadness, just acknowledgement that something had changed. If only Timothy had such an outlook.

"It's not a problem. I'm happy to help." Timothy set his tools down and examined what remained of the shelf. It did not keep his mind from wandering, however. He needed the work. These odd jobs provided for his mother and himself. Barely.

"I got some more boards in the back. I don't reckon this one is salvageable." Mr. Yerby slapped a hand on what remained of the broken piece of wood.

"Don't think so," Timothy muttered.

"I can show you where I keep those things." Mr. Yerby motioned to the rear exit from the building.

Timothy waved a hand. "That's not necessary. Unless you have something you plan to use for another project."

Mr. Yerby shook his head. "Nope."

"Then I think I can figure out something that will work."

Mr. Yerby nodded. "I'll let you get to it. Just holler if you have any questions."

Timothy gripped the splintered board. He needed to gauge how wide and long it was. If he had to cut a board to size, that would take more effort. Best to limit how much of that he had to do.

Mr. Yerby moved off toward the front of the store.

Timothy noted how his steps were less sure. And that he favored his left leg. Was there more going on? Shaking his head, he tried to clear such thoughts. That was no longer any of his business. He must find a way to live in this town without caring so much about the minutiae of the people. Let Wyatt worry about their physical well-being and Reverend Dawson their spiritual lives. Neither was his concern. Not anymore.

Gripping the board on either side of the split part, he carried it out to the back. Just as Mr. Yerby had said, there were quite a few pieces of wood—scraps really—leaning against the back of the building.

Timothy searched and laid hands on several, doing his best to find the right fit. After a few minutes, he made his way through the layers of boards and found one that was reasonably sized...perhaps a good enough length.

Bringing it back into the shop, he had to step around a woman and her daughter, excusing himself as he did so. He was glad he didn't recognize either. Cripple Creek was growing. And the sooner it filled with people who didn't know about his past as 'Reverend Timothy' the better. Just as well, he would prefer if fewer of the townsfolk knew of his history with Katherine.

It had certainly, by now, come to Jane's awareness. If she couldn't pick out the truth from his and Katherine's interaction, certainly Katie would have shared the whole of it. But why did that bother him?

Was there a part of him that wanted to make more of his exchanges with Jane? Of the—dare he admit even to himself—heat between them? Perhaps it was just his imagining...or wishful thinking.

Did he still want the things he had wanted with Katie—a family, a home, someone to love? There was no sense in it.

He held the board up to its new position on the shelving. It was about an inch too long. But of good thickness. However, he had left his saw in the cart. He made a mark on the board where it would need to be cut and stepped outside.

As he did so, he crossed paths with Mayor Jacobson who headed into the General Store after tipping his hat to Timothy.

One more person who had witnessed his shame, betrayed at Katie's hand. Why did that still scar him so? Could he not just move on?

He made short work of trimming the board before slipping back into the store.

"You don't say," Mr. Yerby exclaimed. He and the mayor now stood at the counter, a sack of flour between them.

"Yes. And without a word, too."

Timothy's curiosity was piqued. But he reminded himself that the affairs of the town no longer concerned him. He may not be a man of the cloth anymore, but that didn't mean he wished to be involved in gossip.

Though as he fit the board into its place on the shelf, he couldn't help overhearing.

"Not a word, you say?" Mr. Yerby's voice punctuated the air.

"No, sir. And here we are...our Miss Elston married off and no one to step in at the schoolhouse. How will we find a teacher on such short notice?"

The new teacher had not come on the stage as supposed? Timothy remembered his mother saying that she was due today. What would they do about the children and their education? Surely the town council would send for another teacher. But that could take weeks.

There he was...considering business that was not his to mind. He shook his head and grabbed for a couple of nails.

He focused on getting the nails secured into place, but he heard Katherine's name and paused. Would they truly ask her to fill in? Preposterous!

Making a show of testing the board's attachment to the shelf, he strained his hearing.

"What is her name again?" Mr. Yerby sounded as if he searched for the information. It was difficult to pick up their words.

"Who? Mrs. Sullivan's friend?" The mayor seemed more interested than he might should be.

"Yes. I believe she's some manner of teacher."

"How long will she be visiting? Do you think she'd be interested in stepping in for the meantime?" Jacobson's voice rose, an edge of excitement in his words.

"I don't know. But it couldn't hurt to ask."

What were the chances Jane would take them up on their offer? Would that keep her around town longer?

"I suppose the town council would have to agree. Maybe I can speak with the members informally and make some kind of proposal to the lady." Mayor Jacobson was deep in thought. That much was obvious. And there was a hopefulness as well.

And as much as Timothy hated it, there was a glimmer of hopefulness in him, too.

No, he chided himself. It would be best if she went back to wherever she came from.

But best for who? Was he so taken with her that her very presence threatened his resolve?

He swung the hammer and bit back a howl. In his distraction, he had pinched his thumb between the hammer and nail. How could he be so thoughtless?

Jane sighed as the scent of coffee reached her. Finally, she would have a cup that wasn't strong enough to pour itself. Wyatt sure did like it that way, but Jane preferred a little more flavor and less bite.

Susie's laughter crossed the space of the large room. Her older brother was doing something comical, no doubt. He certainly had a way with his siblings. Always keeping them entertained with his antics.

The young man was what every parent would want in a child. He was engaged, polite, compliant when needed, and adventurously creative.

Jane smiled as she set her gaze on the smaller figures and tried to take in what was happening.

Jack was on his knees but raised up with arms in the air as if at the climax of some fantastical tale.

Susie was riveted on his every word. Her eyes widened and her smile spread across the whole of her face. She adored her brother.

Movement farther in the house drew Jane's focus from the children. Was Kitty about to make an appearance?

Jane turned back to the coffee pot. Just in time, too. It was ready...on the edge of burnt, in fact. She pulled it from the burner and reached for a mug.

The liquid steamed as it hit the cooler interior of the cup. And the scent wafted up as she breathed it in deeply. It was heavenly.

Footfalls told that Kitty neared the great room. Would she want a cup?

Jane set the pot down and looked up as her friend entered with Ellie Mae perched on her hip, rubbing her eyes.

"How was your nap?" Jane put as much lightness in her voice as possible. Especially since she was starting to worry after her friend—more and more each day. Kitty's normal cheery, lively features were drawn and weary. How much of this was normal for a mother of a young child? How much was too much?

Kitty let out a long breath. "Not long enough. The little miss here decided I was done before I thought I was."

Jane frowned. Kitty had been in her room for a couple of hours. How tired was she?

She quickly shook her head to clear such judgments. Jane had never had a small child be so dependent on her for sustenance. There was little room for Jane to make such assumptions.

Jane walked to her friend. "Perhaps I can take her and you can lie back down?"

Kitty gave her a long look, then glanced at Ellie Mae. What was there to consider? If she was as tired as she appeared, she would do well to accept Jane's offer.

"Really. It's okay. I can handle it."

When Kitty looked at her again, her eyes brimmed with tears. "That's so kind. But you are my guest. And you came to spend time with me...not to babysit my children."

Jane set a hand to her friend's arm. "I am here for *you*. If that means I let you get some much-needed sleep, or support you when things are rough, or we have a chat later...it's all the same to me."

The tears that had threatened slipped down Kitty's cheeks. And her chest jumped with barely contained sobs.

Jane plucked Ellie Mae from her arms. "There, now, there is no need for that."

Kitty swiped at her face as the torrent came. "I don't know what's wrong with me."

"There's nothing *wrong* with you. Young children are demanding. Every mom struggles—especially in these early months."

"You think so?" Kitty's eyes were so deeply hopeful that Jane caught her breath.

"I do." Jane pressed a smile onto her face. Though the nagging in the back of her mind also pushed for attention. Was this really all right? Kitty couldn't seem to get enough sleep, she was emotional and teary often...

Maybe Jane should quiet her trepidations and wait to speak to Wyatt. Surely he would know.

"Now, you go rest and I'll keep an eye on this precious bundle." Jane tapped Ellie Mae's nose and offered the child her finger.

Ellie Mae gripped it and smiled.

Kitty cast a longing look to her baby and then across the room to Jack and Susie. "All right. Have Jack wake me if you need anything."

Jane swallowed her concern at Kitty's woefulness. "We'll be fine. You just rest."

Kitty nodded and turned, all but stumbling toward her bedroom.

Jane's face dropped into a frown.

Ellie Mae's gurgling drew her attention back to the moment.

"I guess I'll have to wait on that coffee, won't I?" Jane planted a kiss on the girl's forehead.

"I'll mind her for a bit."

Jane looked up.

Jack had come into the kitchen. His expression portended his confidence, but his eyes...they were just as concerned as Jane was.

"That's not necessary." Jane waved him off. "It can wait."

"Susie's playing with her blocks. Ellie Mae could help me watch her."

Should she let the boy assist her? He was very kind...so much so that she hated to turn him down.

"Very well." She handed the now squirming child over. "But only for a few minutes."

Jack grinned and took his sister back toward the den.

Folding her arms across herself, Jane wondered at the children. Kitty was so blessed. Jane only hoped that her friend could see that even through her tiredness. What would it be like to have such precious little ones? Certainly, Kitty was proud of her family. Would Jane be as tired? Or find energy from somewhere within to keep up with a gaggle of children?

She prayed the latter. For she was convinced that no one wanted to be a mother more. And since it became more and more unlikely Jane was destined for marriage, she did not think children would be part of her future either.

A loud knock sounded on the door.

Jane jerked her attention to it. And then to Jack.

He shrugged and turned back to his sisters.

Jane ran a hand over her hair, ensuring that all was in place. Then she straightened her shirt and moved in that direction.

"Who is it?" she called as she neared.

"Mayor Jacobson," came the reply.

She had not met the mayor, though Kitty had pointed him out at the wedding festivities. Should she let him in? Maybe once she told him Kitty was unavailable, he'd leave a message and not insist on being let in.

Jane gripped the latch and opened the door only enough for the mayor to see her. "Good day, Mayor Jacobson. I'm Jane Millington, a friend of Kat—er, Katherine. But I'm afraid you have missed her. She is not available at the moment. And Wyatt is at the clinic."

"Oh." The mayor fingered his hat brim. Was he put out? Or nervous? "Sorry to have missed Mrs. Sullivan."

"I'll let her know you stopped by." Jane started to close the door.

But Mayor Jacobson halted the door's progress. "Actually..."

Jane jerked back. What did the man want?

"I was hoping to speak with *you*."

Now that was surprising. Her? What could the mayor want with her? But she no longer pushed on the door.

"May I...come in?" The mayor slanted to try to look inside as the sounds of laughter from the children spread through the area.

Jane's initial reaction was to grip the door tighter to keep it only slightly open. But she caught herself. Was there any reason she should not trust this man? Perhaps not. But she still struggled with the fact that she didn't know if this man really was who he said he was. Maybe she could step out onto the porch? But that would leave the children unattended.

"Perhaps it would be best if we just chatted here."

Mayor Jacobson quirked a brow but settled back on his heels all the same. "Very well. I have come to...offer you a proposal."

She had heard of men out West being desperate for a wife, but this? Her head spun. "Excuse me?"

Whether it was the reaction on her face or something else, she didn't know. But he tried to retract his offer.

"I-I mean, a job offer."

Job? What was this man about?

"I'm sorry, Mr. Jacobson, but I really should get back to the—"

He held up a hand. "I'm not making myself very clear, am I?"

She watched him warily but did not shut the door...yet.

"It seems our teacher decided not to come to Cripple Creek. And we find ourselves in a bind. The school year is about to start and we are without someone to mind the children."

Jane stared. He couldn't really be offering her the position, could he? Were they so desperate they'd reach out to any single, educated woman in the region?

The mayor rushed on. "I understand that you may not have planned such an extended stay. This would be a temporary arrangement. Until another teacher could be found."

That helped the knot in Jane's chest loosen a bit. But could she abandon Kat, what with her fatigue and moodiness?

The mayor's features took on a pleading look. "Please don't say 'no' without thinking on it."

Jane chewed on her lip.

"I don't mean to be pressing you for an answer this second. Just... think about it." With that, Mayor Jacobson put on his hat and stepped back. "You can find me around town."

Jane remained glued to the spot, not sure how to react. She should refuse right here and now. But she couldn't make herself say the words.

"I'll take my leave, then. It was good to meet you, Miss Millington. Goodbye, kids," he hollered.

"Bye, Mr. Jacobson," Jack called from within.

Jane's face warmed as she closed the door and stepped back toward the kitchen. Well, she *never* would have expected such in a hundred years. And just what was she going to do about it? She felt oddly guilty about not helping when she was fully capable and not otherwise engaged—by a job or a prospective husband. Was this, then, her purpose? To serve the children of this town? Or was there the possibility of more to her sad life?

She picked up her mug...finally.

Took a sip, and grimaced. The coffee had grown cold.

Timothy reached up to steady his mother's awkward dismount from the driver's box.

"Easy," he admonished. The woman didn't seem to fully understand her own mobility issues. There was little good that might come from her dropping down as if she were much younger.

With effort, Timothy managed to get her to the ground. By the time he accomplished it, his thumb throbbed. He had bandaged it, but it still smarted.

How would they continue like this? Mother's shaky hands and strength challenges had already limited her ability to midwife. How much longer would it be before she was unable to do normal things? He didn't want to think about that. But he must.

She still gripped his shoulders.

He looked down into her deep brown eyes. There was a trepidation there, a hesitation. As if she knew.

"Thank you," she murmured. Was she so embarrassed by her own limitations? Was there anything he could do or say to assuage it?

"Why don't I walk you to the General Store?" He took her arm and angled her that way.

"I'm quite certain I can manage..." she started, pulling back a bit.

He had to come up with an excuse then. "I need to check that shelf Mr. Yerby had me repair. I want to see that it's holding up well enough."

She patted the side of his face. "Such a good boy."

He reached up and took her hand, placing it on his arm. While he didn't enjoy these moments, he allowed it because he also knew they wouldn't last.

Steering her away from the cart, he aimed for the mercantile establishment. Could he leave her there to shop? Perhaps not. But he didn't want to linger either. Nor rush her.

He sighed as they crossed the threshold into the store.

"Timothy," Mr. Yerby called from behind the counter. "Mrs. Johnson."

"Morning," Mother said as she slipped her arm from Timothy's.

He reached out to steady her but let his hand fall to his side.

"That shelf has never been better," Mr. Yerby said before turning and nodding at an approaching customer.

"Glad to hear it." Timothy watched his mother walk farther into the store. She was sure on her feet, but he did wonder after her. Should he stay? Or give her the independence due her?

The woman at the counter turned toward him. It was Mrs. Smith, the livery owner's wife. "How good to see you out and about, Reverend."

He cringed. "It's just Timothy now." How many times would he have to remind these people? And why did he feel it necessary to correct her?

"My apologies," she said, a frown crossing her features.

The air had a tension to it. Did he have to create such strain with his insistence?

"Will that be all?" Mr. Yerby broke the silence.

Timothy wanted to thank the man for coming to his aid.

"Ah, yes," Mrs. Smith laid her shopping basket on the surface separating her from Mr. Yerby. "I didn't know you had more of that blackberry jam."

Mrs. Smith and Mr. Yerby continued their conversation. And Timothy looked to where his mother had gone. She chatted with another woman by the fabric. But the woman's back was to him and her hat shielded her face. It was no matter.

Perhaps he might leave Mother to her shopping and grab a cup of coffee at the café. Decided, he slipped from the store and ducked his head as he moved down the planked sidewalk.

As he passed the alleyway, however, he heard a *chink* of something hitting the side of the building. He looked up.

The boy that had been harassing the lizard a few days ago stood in the alley, having just thrown something farther back.

Timothy's gaze darted in that direction in time to see two cats scurry away.

Had the boy intentionally thrown the rock at them? For what purpose? Timothy frowned, there was no good reason for such.

He stepped into the space between the buildings, approaching the boy. "What are you doing?" He tried to keep his voice nonthreatening, yet commanding.

The boy turned, there was a redness about his eyes. Had he been crying? His features contorted into a glower. "Leave me alone."

He attempted to run past Timothy, but Timothy caught him. "Wait a minute."

"Let me go!"

"Just a second, young man." Timothy ducked to look the boy in the face.

His features were a mask of anger. But there was pain there, too.

"Why are you trying to scare the poor cats?"

The boy huffed.

Timothy turned the boy to face him as he crouched. "Where are your parents?"

The boy's hardened expression cracked and his eyes reflected a certain fear about them. Would he refuse to respond?"

"Listen..." Timothy knew that fear. He had witnessed it many times in the face of his one-time friend, Wyatt. The doctor's father had not hesitated to work his anger upon his son. Was this boy in a similar situation? "I'm not aiming to get you into trouble."

The boy's eyebrows lifted. Would he trust Timothy?

"I think we have gotten off on the wrong foot." Timothy relaxed his hold. "I'm Timothy Johnson. And I—"

"I know who you are." The boy seemed as if he were rising to challenge Timothy.

"All right." Timothy kept his tone light. "But I'm afraid I don't know who you are."

The boy kicked at a rock near his foot.

Timothy pushed out a breath. "Look, I'm trying here."

The lad's expression betrayed a hint of curiosity. "My name's Lemuel."

Did Lemuel avoid sharing his surname on purpose? That didn't deter Timothy.

"I was headed to the café. Want to join me? That is...if it's all right with your parents."

Lemuel looked off somewhere behind Timothy but didn't say anything.

Timothy turned. The boy stared at the saloon. Is that where his Pa was? Had the man no care for what trouble his boy could get into while he drowned himself in drink?

What about the boy's mother? Was she home? Or gone—dead or otherwise departed?

When he looked back at the boy, Lemuel's trepidation made his turmoil and pain more evident. And Timothy was sure his mother was no longer in the picture.

"If you don't think your Pa would mind, I'll get you a slice of Mrs. Abby's apple pie. Would you like that?"

Lemuel seemed to consider it. Then frowned. "I don't know."

"You know, Mrs. Abby's pies are the finest in the whole of Colorado."

It was obvious the boy wanted the pie. But worried about his father's reaction. Though Timothy knew it was unlikely the man would be concerned about his son. If he had any awareness when he left the saloon.

"It won't take long. Maybe you could eat the pie outside on the boardwalk...in case your Pa gets done with whatever is keeping him."

The boy met Timothy's gaze. He was sold.

Timothy wished he could offer the boy more than just a slice of pie, but that was what he could do for now.

Lemuel nodded.

The pair moved off toward the café. And Timothy was once again unsure of himself. Should he let the boy be? Or try to make conversation?

Either way, Lemuel was unlikely to answer and Timothy didn't feel much like pleasantries. So, silence it was.

As they neared the eatery, Timothy stepped to the side to allow other patrons to exit.

The couple emerging nodded to Timothy and kept moving.

He motioned to Lemuel and they stepped toward the door.

Only to collide with another exiting figure.

Timothy reached out to steady the smaller frame. And found himself staring into the eyes of Miss Jane Millington.

CHAPTER 5

Contention

J ane jerked back from the solid wall she had hit. What just happened? She stared up into warm brown eyes. Timothy? "Pardon me!"

His hands were on her arms, steadying her. Should she pull back? Something told her yes, but she didn't move.

"Are you all right?"

"Yes," she said, "I...ah...I'm sorry for nearly running you over. My mind must be somewhere else."

"It's nothing to worry about."

The calmness of his tone belied the moment. And the way they had last parted. What was going on in his mind? Did he remember storming off? Or did other thoughts flit through his head? The kind that filled her with the oddly comforting sensations pulsing within. Fluttering in her stomach dashed any hope she had of forming a complete thought. Why did he have to be so kind? And quite fit. Though her hands gripped only his arms, she noted the firmness of the muscles in his upper arms. Not at all what she had expected.

"You okay, miss?" Another voice broke into her thoughts.

She turned. It was a boy that had to be ten or so. He stared at her, a look of confusion about him. Why?

Then she realized that she still leaned on Timothy. It must seem odd indeed.

She extracted herself from his strong arms. But not without regret. And ran her hands down the front of her dress to straighten herself. "Yes. That is, I'm quite well, I assure you."

Timothy's eyes danced and a smile played at the corners of his mouth. Could he read her thoughts? Did he know that she had lost herself so completely? It had only been a handful of seconds surely.

"Care to join us?" Timothy offered, indicating the café. His features told that his words surprised even him a bit. What was that?

The lad made an exasperated sound.

But when she met Timothy's gaze again, she found herself muttering, "I wish I could. I am...um...looking for Mayor Jacobson."

Timothy frowned. Did he dislike the mayor? Or was something else at play here?

"Lemuel, why don't you run along into the café and order that pie?" Timothy dug in his pocket and produced a couple of coins that he pressed into the boy's hand.

The lad looked at his fisted hand then at Timothy...almost as if he didn't trust something about the situation. Was it her? But he relented and sped on into the café without further delay.

Timothy turned his attention back to her. "I've just gotten to town myself. Not sure where the mayor is, but he's usually about this time of day."

Jane frowned. "I've searched the mercantile, the livery, the café... I'm not quite certain where else to look."

"I can tell him you're looking for him." Timothy swallowed. Was he nervous about something? It seemed so. "Is there, ah, a message I can give him?"

Jane looked at her hands settled in front of her. "It's not something I..."

He watched her struggle for words. "Oh, I don't mean to intrude. Especially if it's personal." Then he turned toward the café.

"It's not," she blurted out as she grabbed for his arm. She jerked back as he turned, almost as if touching him singed her. Indeed, it did send warm tingles up her arm. For whatever reason, she wanted him to know there was nothing intimate about her request to speak with the mayor. Nor was she prepared to end their exchange.

She had thought of him often since the wedding. Mostly about whatever might have injured him so that he would walk away like he did. Kitty had been less forthcoming on that matter when questioned. She had all but brushed Jane off.

Timothy looked at her hand so near his arm. She imagined that he, too, was affected by her touch. Then she shook her head. That was silliness. Such an imagination she had.

His eyes met hers. And his gaze became intense.

For whatever reason, she felt compelled to fill the silence. "I...have been offered a temporary teaching position at the school."

She wanted him to be...what? Pleased? Hopeful? He didn't appear at all concerned one way or the other. It deflated her a bit.

"Only until the new teacher comes," she rushed on to say, her face heating. Why was she telling him all of this?

"Oh." His gaze darted here and there. "I'm sure you have...things calling you back home to..."

As his voice trailed, she realized they had not been acquainted enough for him to know such a detail. "San Francisco."

He nodded. His eyes held a mystery. What did he feel? If anything. And again she chastised herself for her fanciful thoughts.

"You must have a beau, or family waiting back in California."

She shook her head. "No." Then she considered the word. "I actually don't. No one is waiting for me but an empty boarding house room."

"Oh?" His tone rose.

Was it her imaginings or did he seem the slightest bit hopeful? Maybe it was nothing more than his desire to end this interaction.

She had planned to tell the mayor that she couldn't commit. Her stay in Cripple Creek was just not supposed to be extended. And she had to return... But to what? No one and nothing would be there for her. What pulled her from this opportunity to help this town, get a paying interim job, and spend more time with Kat?

"You're still out here talking?" It was the boy, Lemuel. He emerged from the café with a piece of pie in hand. He moved off to sit on the edge of the boardwalk some several feet down.

It occurred to her that Timothy may have some connection to him. Was this a nephew? The son of a friend? Or...his son?

She didn't know. The heat in her face burned hotter. "I really must be going." Stepping forward to move past him, she tried to avoid his gaze.

"Hope you find the mayor." His words were plain, uncertain. "If I see him, I'll let him know."

"Thank you, sir." She moved off down the boardwalk, forcing herself to not look back.

She was certainly and most desperately hopeless.

How could a thumb hurt so much? Timothy had not had much occasion to nurse an injury. But he never would have expected his minor mishap to lead to this.

Grumbling, he dismounted in the center of Cripple Creek's main stretch. He had avoided the clinic at all costs since Wyatt and Katherine...since before Timothy's return. Facing off with his one-time friend who had betrayed him just didn't sit well. Not then, and not now.

But how was he to escape it? His mother had tended Timothy's wound as best she could. Which was not much more than he had done for himself—a thorough wash and bandage. Still, the injury had become increasingly painful as the days passed. Enough so that he feared he might lose the thumb or risk more if the infection spread.

As much as it hurt his pride to show up at Wyatt's clinic, he was not ignorant or reckless.

He stepped closer to the door, hoping that there would be others within. This was one time he preferred not to have privacy for treatment. He had a thought to pray, but quickly dismissed that. There had not been the compulsion to pray in some time. And the longer he avoided it, the less he felt the urge to.

Taking a deep breath, he knocked on the clinic door.

A voice came from within. "Be there in just a minute!"

It was Wyatt. He didn't have to see the man to know that it was him. And it wasn't as if he expected anyone else. Though perhaps he had wished to delay this visit, even if only for a day, if Wyatt had been unavailable. He had already put it off because of the rain earlier. If his mother hadn't pestered him so, he would have let it excuse him doing this tomorrow.

What would his former friend say when he answered the door? Timothy trusted the man to be diligent and capable no matter what tension lay between them. Yes, Wyatt would do his job to the best of his ability. Besides, it wasn't as if Timothy had wronged him.

Not truly.

That whole interaction with Katie after they were married had been innocent—one friend offering a shoulder to help another through a tough time.

Timothy sighed. It was forgivable. Especially since nothing had really happened.

His thoughts tugged at him, and a nagging guilt pulled at his heart. But did he deserve that? After all, he had been the one wronged. With Wyatt proposing to Katie while Timothy was courting her. As if that weren't bad enough, they snuck off and got married! No, Timothy refused to own any remorse for wrongs he did not commit.

The door opened before he followed that thought.

Wyatt's features appeared to strain. "Something I can help you with, Timothy?"

How he wished that Wyatt didn't need to address him so. This was the one time he had wished for his former title of 'reverend,' if for no other reason, than to put some emotional distance between them.

Timothy tried to look farther into the clinic. Was Katie here? That would be the height of discomfort for him. But his efforts were in vain. Wyatt only held the door open far enough for him to look out.

Best to get it over with. "I...seem to have injured my thumb."

Wyatt's gaze settled on Timothy's raised hand. "Let's take a look at it." He pulled the door open wider and ushered Timothy in.

The tentative steps Timothy took into the clinic were measured and hesitant.

Wyatt had already moved across the room to his wash basin. "Please, have a seat on the exam table."

Timothy eyed the surface. He remembered when Katie had been injured on one of their walks and he brought her here. And then his visits to see her when she had the typhoid. She had been so fragile. On the edge of life and death. Emotions poured through him—feelings he would rather keep in check.

Wyatt dried his hands with a towel by the basin. Turning and finding Timothy still just inside the door, his brow lifted. "You all right?"

Timothy swallowed. "Yes. Just the thumb." He stepped to the exam table and settled on it. Not overly comfortable, but more so than it appeared.

Wyatt came to where Timothy sat. "I'll just remove this bandage." He reached for the cloth strip.

Timothy jerked away. "I can manage."

Wyatt's eyes widened just slightly.

Why did he have to make things worse? Timothy worked on the bandage as he grimaced. More from the tension than the pain. Again, it wasn't as if Timothy had anything to feel bad about. Wyatt and Katie had wronged *him*. Not the other way around.

Wyatt watched as Timothy finished taking off the ragged cloth strips.

"Yeah. That's infected."

Yes, Timothy had figured as much. Instead of barking back a sharp retort, he nodded.

"I have a salve I want you to be sure to put on it. And keep it clean."

Why had Timothy come again? For this useless advice?

"I will have to see you back in three days. If it has not improved at all, I'll have to open it to wash the infection out."

Timothy fought the urge to look in Wyatt's direction. Open it? That did not sound pleasant.

Wyatt moved toward the cabinet where he kept his medicinals. "You'll have to be careful to clean and dress it with fresh bandages a couple times a day."

Timothy nodded though Wyatt couldn't see him, his attention on the contents of the cabinet and his back to Timothy.

He stared at the doctor. Wishing he could hurl something at him. Wyatt acted as though there was nothing going on here. As if he had absolved himself of any wrongdoing.

What could Timothy say? What could he do that would levy guilt upon Wyatt without actually speaking of it?

Wyatt handed him a tin.

Ah, yes. The salve.

"Check back in on Wednesday."

Timothy nodded again, still mulling over his options. There didn't seem to be space for him to accuse Wyatt of anything. Nor did he believe there any benefit to that. So he took the tin, opened it, and rubbed some on his thumb.

The door opened.

Timothy jerked his head that way in time to see Katie walk in. His heart stopped.

"Wyatt, I'm worried about Jane, she..." Her voice trailed as her gaze settled on Timothy.

Timothy grabbed for his used bandage.

Wyatt stepped toward Katie. "What's the matter with Jane?"

Did Katie say Jane? Was Jane in some kind of trouble? His thoughts of the thick tension in the room melted into worry.

Katie glared at him, but he moved around the opposite side of the exam table to avoid crossing her path.

"Katie?" Wyatt prodded.

She seemed to come back around to herself. "Jane hasn't returned from the schoolhouse. Jack came home over an hour ago. We went to check on her, and she's not there anymore. Something's happened, I know it!"

Timothy fought down the urge to ask questions. There was no reason he should be concerned or even care. That might mean his heart was more involved than he dare allow it.

Wyatt and Katherine continued their discussion, trying to figure out what to do. It was simple enough for Timothy to excuse himself quietly. They likely didn't even notice.

He hastily wrapped his thumb again as he put the tin in his saddlebag.

What had happened to Jane? Where could she be? Was something more wrong here?

He pushed those thoughts to the side. It was none of his business. None of his concern in the least.

Besides, he was needed at home.

He lifted himself into the saddle and with a last look at the clinic, he jerked the reins in the opposite direction.

Jane lay in thick, mired earth. What had happened? One second she had been trying to urge the horse to keep going despite the mud, and the next she woke on the ground. Had the horse been spooked? Slipped in the loose ground? She couldn't seem to figure it out. It didn't help that nothing looked clear to her. A blurred haze had fallen over everything.

Fine independent woman she made. Only one day of class and she couldn't even manage to get herself back to Kitty's home.

What would her aunt think of her now? She'd likely be just as disappointed as she always was. But now most certainly. *A woman should be able to stand on her own, without the need of a man.* Had the woman felt that way because she'd been hurt or because she had such an independent streak? Jane had never puzzled that one out. Either way, Jane always felt as if she were nothing more than a bother.

She shifted, but an ache in her head forced her to stop. Had she been injured?

Looking around, she attempted to find the horse. It was nowhere to be seen.

What was she supposed to do now? She was in the middle of the washed-out path. Had she even been on the right one? Her surroundings did not look familiar. Hadn't for the last bit. She had to face the truth: she was lost. Injured...and lost.

For how long? And what would befall her? She was defenseless and alone.

Emotion tightened her throat as intense fear filled her. No, she would not let herself give into this.

Clomping of hooves thundered the ground. Was this friend or foe? Someone who would mean her harm? She didn't know whether to cry out and make her presence known or pray they passed on.

But the sound became louder. Indeed whoever it was moved about as if searching. Dare she hope it was Kitty or Wyatt or maybe the mayor looking for her?

After some back and forth in the area, the hoofbeats were surer and nearer.

"Jane?" The familiar voice was a heavenly sound.

"Timothy?" she called, hearing the waver in her voice as she did so. "I'm here."

She spotted him as he appeared in her periphery. Turning her head in that direction, she thanked the Lord for His provision.

"Are you all right?" Timothy's voice was strained as he dismounted and stepped closer.

"I think so." Jane seethed despite her attempt to maintain her hold on her emotions.

Timothy frowned. At least it seemed as if he did. Oh, why wouldn't the world be still? Everything danced and swirled. Or perhaps it was her vision.

Timothy's calm words filled the gap between them again. "It doesn't seem so. Don't try to move. I'm coming."

She could do nothing but wait as he moved toward her position. While she wanted to raise herself up and prove she could handle the pain, the dizziness prevented her from trying. Lifting a hand to press to her forehead did not improve her situation.

Then a touch, gentle and searching, fell on her wrist.

She startled, jerking back to find that Timothy now hovered over her. His deep brown eyes radiated concern.

At her reaction, he frowned. "It's just me. I'm going to get you out of here."

That was why he was here, wasn't it? And she thanked the Lord he had passed this way and found her before a wild creature or someone with less noble intentions. Yet, her eyes filled with emotion.

"Don't." He gripped her hand. "I'm here." He settled onto the ground next to her, his eyes never leaving her face.

She bit at her lip to stop the release of the torrent within, but it did not help. Tears slid down her cheeks.

He lowered his free hand to rub them away, cupping her face and stroking with the pads of his thumbs, though one was bandaged.

"I..." She couldn't manage anything further with the tightness in her throat.

"There is no need." His voice was strong, sure.

As if it was all she needed to hold to. Indeed, the pain seemed to ease a bit as her vision focused on him. Only him.

She had the thought that she should be embarrassed, yet she

wasn't, lost in his eyes as she was. Had they always held such depth and fullness? His gaze on her was tender and warm. If only she could tuck herself there and rest. A good, long, much desperately needed rest.

"You're shaking." His words were soft and still laced with apprehension. For her?

She only then noticed that her hands trembled.

He broke contact with her for a moment as he slid his jacket off. Then he lifted her into his arms, cradling her as he wrapped his coat around her.

She wanted to look away. Tried to no avail. But his pull was too great. As was her own pleasure at the depth of his concern for her. Had anyone ever cared so much? Why would he?

He tucked her closer, but she resisted losing eye contact and kept her head enough off his shoulder to maintain it.

His breaths quickened slightly and his pupils dilated. Because of her? Did he feel this thing between them? For a heat not due to his coat's added layers penetrated her being, settling in her core, stirring sensations through her that could not be explained any other way— she cared for him, too. Perhaps more than she should.

"Jane," came his harsh whisper. Yet her name on his lips was the sweetest sound she'd ever heard.

She wanted to say something, but the pooling sensations flared out in her chest, stealing her senses. Without inhibition, she slid a hand to his face. Her fingers seemed to have a mind of their own as they traced the roughness of his jaw.

Then she noticed how dirt-marred her hands were. Why would he allow her to touch him thusly?

She drew her hand back. "I'm sorry. I didn't intend to…"

And once again, she lost her words as her gaze slid back to his eyes. There was a desire there. For what? For her? Or was it only physical attraction? Did she care? In that moment, all she could think about was what it might feel like for his lips to press to hers.

The next moment, her gaze drifted to his mouth, unbidden, uncontrolled. She must contain herself! She was foolish...these thoughts, these desires. He had made himself very clear, had he not?

But in this moment, nothing seemed clear beyond her want of him.

His eyes fell to her lips.

Hers parted as if prepared to receive his affection. Did she have no more control than this? She opened herself up to ridicule and rejection.

He leaned forward. Would he kiss her? It seemed a far-flung hope, yet his face came ever closer to hers.

His gaze found hers again. Did he seek permission?

How was one to give it in such a space?

He halted but an inch from her. This was madness. Why did he deny her? Or did he invite her?

Throwing caution to the side, she gripped his shirt front and closed the small gap between them.

She had intended to satisfy her curiosity as to how his lips might feel.

But the moment she touched his lips, his mouth sealed the kiss.

Her stomach fluttered and a warmth swirled through her.

But it wasn't enough.

She leaned back against his arms, sure that would break the spell.

"Jane," he murmured as he followed her, slanting his mouth over her lips again, pressing into her, pulling her closer. As if he were so ravenous for her.

She responded as well as she could, mimicking his movements and the way his mouth caressed hers.

How long the kiss lingered was unclear. When he did release her lips, she was breathless.

He drew his face back from hers, but then set his forehead against hers.

"I..." he attempted to say something, but it didn't come. Did he mean to apologize? Excuse himself for being caught up in the moment? Would such a confession break this moment and halt the waves of heat buffeting her heart?

She set a hand to his face again, sliding a thumb over his mouth. "Don't," she managed.

Their breaths were coming in gasps.

He moved her hand from his face. "You are not yourself," he said. "I am a brute."

She opened her eyes, wanting to stop him. Wanting him to refrain from saying any more. Everything in her needed him to want whatever this was between them. Releasing a sigh, she knew she could not make it true. No matter how much she wished for it.

"I...seem to be a bit out of sorts," she said, letting him pull back.

He nodded. But the wideness of his eyes gave her pause. Were his words testing out how much she wanted his kiss?

"Let me get you into town. But I need to know what hurts before I try to move you." His words were both measured and stuttered. As if he had lost his hold on his emotions as well. Or was that only her wanting to see something that wasn't there?

"I am sore. That is all. Perhaps bruised, but not broken." She wished she could speak the same of her heart, which felt as if it were ripping in two.

He nodded, his eyes not yet moving from her face.

Perhaps there was hope. He would not look at her this way if he didn't care, right? She was sure he did. She had felt it.

He braced himself and lifted her as he stood, his gaze averting to their surroundings.

She felt the loss of the connection as keenly as if he'd sliced it with a knife. And she knew she was far too much of a hopeless case.

Loosening her hold from his shirt front, she tucked her hands deeper into his jacket.

He moved to his horse and helped her into the saddle.

As he set himself to mounting the horse, she felt every bit the loss of his presence. And her own shame.

How could she have been so caught up? She was certainly conjuring that his reaction to her meant more.

Still, she burrowed her face into his jacket and breathed in the scent of him, lingering in their embrace, their intimate kiss a little bit longer. Despite what her aunt may have thought or believed, Jane wanted this. This and so much more.

CHAPTER 6

Uncertain

Timothy stared at the boards beneath his feet as he paced. How had he found himself at the clinic not once, but twice this day?

It didn't matter. All he cared about was Wyatt opening that door and pronouncing that Jane was well and would recover fully.

As it was, Timothy waited. And paced.

How could this have happened? He found himself once again at the mercy of his more tender feelings. He never should have kissed her. That had been a mistake.

Though it hadn't felt that way. It seemed like the most real and reasonable thing to do in the moment. He had wanted to. Plain and simple.

Had she wanted him to? It had seemed so. The way she had melted to him. And her lips had been so soft...heavenly. It brought something to life in him. Something long buried.

But did that mean he should have done it?

Absolutely not. There was one thing he would agree with Scripture about to this day—the heart was deceitful. Had he not learned that lesson well enough with Katherine? Had the months following her and Wyatt's wedding not taught him as much? Days and nights of trying to forget. Of striving to find healing for his heart.

No, clearly not.

"Timothy, calm yourself. You'll wear your shoes out."

The voice made him cringe. Katherine.

As if this whole situation wasn't bad enough, he waited out here with *her*.

He had rushed Jane to town and soon after, men from the town had found Wyatt on his own search for Jane. Now, there was nothing to do but wait for his pronouncement.

"Timothy," Katherine beseeched him again.

He paused and fought the desire to shoot her a hard look. It wasn't her fault he kissed Jane, had let himself feel for Jane.

"What?" His voice was more subdued than he'd expected.

"You care for her, don't you?" Katherine's words didn't accuse or push, but they were simple and gentle.

He jerked his head to face her, eyes widening. How could it be that others could see, could know? Hadn't he just now come to acknowledge it?

This must end.

"Don't let the wounds of the past keep you from finding happiness."

How dare she speak so soothingly. Did she know how her words condescended? How they bit at him?

But again, he sucked in his response with a breath. He would not be baited.

Looking across the main stretch, the saloon had never appealed as much as it did in that moment, with his heart bleeding out. And his inability to contain it.

"I wish you knew how sorry I am." Katherine seemed to choke on the words.

As much as he wanted to therefore dismiss them, he knew it was not that. She did regret it. He might not want to believe it, but he knew she did. That wasn't the problem.

He folded arms across his chest and kept his gaze trained on the swinging doors of the establishment nearby.

"Can you forgive me?"

Timothy whirled on her then. Forgive her? He was so stunned by her words that he couldn't put two thoughts together. Not even to form a sentence.

The door to the clinic opened, cutting off more words between them.

Wyatt stepped out. He looked between Timothy and Katherine. No doubt he sensed the tense moment. Did he think more of it than he should?

"How is she?" It was Katherine who found her voice first.

"She's fine. Resting. I think it would be best if we watch her closely for the next couple of days. Head injuries can be tricky to manage. And even harder to know exactly what's going on."

Timothy nodded and glanced back to the planks that made up the walkway.

"She is..." Wyatt cleared his throat. "Asking for you."

Timothy looked up. Wyatt was staring at him. Did Jane want to see him? Not Katherine, but him?

It was too much. This felt too deeply involved.

He shouldn't have lingered, no matter how difficult it would have been to leave and not know.

"You can go in and see her now." Wyatt's words were flat and uncertain.

Timothy looked to Katie. Her eyes were expectant, knowing. Or at least he thought she did.

And, in that moment, he knew he had to get out of there. He wouldn't risk himself again. He couldn't. So he turned without a word and walked away.

Jane worked to dress herself. She had been cooped up for too long. It had only been a few days, but that was a few days too many.

She buttoned her shirt as her thoughts went through her rescue for the hundredth time. Timothy had been so wonderful. Then he hadn't come to see her. Maybe he didn't care. Maybe she had forced the intimacy. Maybe her aunt had been right all along.

Wiping an errant tear, she chided herself. She couldn't lose it. Not here. Not when Wyatt was letting her return to the Sullivan homestead. And the school.

A part of her worried after another incident, but she wouldn't give over to that concern.

Besides, the mayor would be here in a few moments to go with her to the schoolhouse. She had asked if she could show him a few of the things she noticed. The building was in much need of repair. Had the previous teacher not cared? Or...had her requests fallen on deaf ears?

Jane found that difficult to believe. The mayor seemed like a reasonable man. And she had no doubt the town council was as well.

Her clothes in place, she checked her hair one last time and stepped into the main clinic area.

Wyatt was already moving about, checking the things in his cabinet. He was meticulous.

"Good morning," she managed. There was a small fear in her that he wouldn't, after all, release her to regular activity today.

"Good morning," he said as he tossed a look over his shoulder. "You still feeling up to it?"

She nodded. "I'm quite well enough I think."

He closed the cabinet and stepped to his desk across the room. "Very well. Would you like some coffee?"

"Did you make it?" The words were out of her mouth before she could stop them. She shook her head. "I don't mean any offense."

His smile told that her comment instead amused. "No. Mrs. Abby is bringing over some breakfast and coffee for you."

"Oh. Thank you. But I have an appointment with Mayor Jacobson." She hoped Wyatt wouldn't restrict her from the short walk to the schoolhouse.

"Oh?" He quirked an eyebrow.

"Yes. I mentioned before when he was here that the school has some maintenance needs."

"Ah." He looked at a couple of papers. "I suppose I'll have to find a way to make use of that food so Mrs. Abby won't be sore at me."

"Will she be?" Jane couldn't discern from his tone if he were kidding.

"No." He looked up, and she could then see his half smile. "I can make use of it all right." A quick pat on his stomach solidified his meaning.

Jane relaxed. She wanted to ask after Timothy again but could not think of how to do so without sounding pushy. How did a woman ask for the tenth time without seeming desperate?

She sighed. There was no point. If Timothy had wanted to see her, he would have found a way.

Maybe he feared he had given her the wrong impression. Or felt bad that he had let her kiss him and carry on like a ninny.

Perhaps it was best. She would have been frightful embarrassed to face him either way.

A knock on the door dispelled her racing thoughts.

"That should be Mayor Jacobson," she said, stepping toward the door.

Indeed, the mayor stood on the other side. "Good morning, Miss Millington. I trust that you are well today."

"Yes. I'm quite well."

The mayor looked over at Wyatt as if he needed the doctor's assessment.

Jane was rather taken off balance. Did she not have the ability to determine her own wellbeing?

She let the whole thing slide, though. There was no need to challenge the man when she needed his willingness to help.

Wyatt all but ignored the mayor, continuing to leaf through papers.

The mayor let out a breath and turned back to Jane. "Shall we, then?"

She nodded, grabbing for her coat and stepping outside.

The mayor held up an arm. "Ladies first."

She stepped past him and moved down the main stretch and past the General Store. Once they passed it, the schoolhouse was a short walk from there.

As they approached, Jane began to feel uncomfortable. Her head throbbed slightly and she questioned her urge to be up and about.

Pushing the discomfort to the side, she reached for the latch and let the mayor into the schoolhouse, careful to keep the door wide open for propriety's sake.

Mayor Jacobson took off his hat and surveyed the one room school. His gaze moved between the leaky roof, to the hole in the floor, to the banged-up woodstove. "I haven't been in here for quite some time. Miss Elston never wanted interference from the council. And she never mentioned any of these things. I had no idea the schoolhouse was in such a state."

The man truly seemed embarrassed by what he found. Jane believed he didn't know.

"The question is not so much how did it get this way...as much as what can be done to repair it?" Jane never did see the point in focusing on the problem. Seeking solutions seemed the most logical approach. Always.

"I...can't rightly say at the moment." His attention was hard to hold because his eyes swept the room repeatedly.

"How am I supposed to teach in these conditions? How are the children supposed to learn when they are cold and wet?"

The mayor grimaced. "I assure you, Miss Millington, we will address this immediately. There are a few men in town that can make these repairs. We'll see who can start on them today." He looked to the roof. "I am altogether certain that whole thing will have to be replaced."

"It was in a state already, but that rainstorm made it worse."

The rainstorm that had found her injured and in Timothy's arms.

Her face heated. Now was not the time for that.

"I thank you, Mayor, for your care and consideration. And the quicker these things can be done, the better."

"Agreed." He couldn't stop looking at the roof, it seemed. "If you will help my wife make a list of the repairs and maintenance needed, I will get the council to vote on it. But we will get someone in here to work on this roof today if possible."

She released her tension. "Thank you." Jane wasn't sure what she had expected...perhaps some pushback, but the man was rather reasonable after all.

"For now, let's head back. I need to make some inquiries."

She nodded and let him usher her out of the shambled room.

At least something was going right.

Timothy's arms ached from his ever-increasing chores around the homestead. But with Ma's health as such, what could he do? Shutting the horse's stall once more, he gripped the shovel in his injured hand, thankful that the thumb had much improved. It enabled him to get back to the more intricate tasks. And back to work. Funds were such that they were much in need of an influx of money. Best not to dwell too much on that, however.

Actually, today was the day he was supposed to return to the clinic for Wyatt to check on him. But he hadn't. And he had no plans to. His thumb was better. Why chance another uncomfortable several minutes with Wyatt and the trouble of going to town to hear what he already knew?

Part of him felt guilty. Wyatt had helped him. Wasn't following instructions the least he could do?

No, he didn't owe anyone anything.

He sighed as he set the shovel back in its place. There was no escaping that the real reason he avoided the clinic this time was the chance he would cross paths with Jane. It wasn't right. It may not be fair. But it was.

How could he put himself in that position...seeing her, being around her, the lightest taste of this dream he would never—could never—have?

Timothy closed the barn doors and moved toward the house that had been his home since before he could remember. The house his father had lovingly built for his bride. That thought brought with it a swell of emotion. Because he still missed his father? Or because he was determined that such would never be his?

He didn't know and he didn't linger on it.

Pushing the front door open, he scanned the large room. Mother was at the stove, dumping spices into a pot. The pungent smell of sage hit him. It was a bit overwhelming.

"What's cooking?" Timothy spoke loudly. He did not want to startle his mother.

She jerked at his words. "Goodness me." Her hand pressed to her chest. "Must you?"

He frowned but soon let out a breath. There was no hope there. No matter what he did, it didn't seem he could avoid such.

"I'm making chili." She turned back toward the steaming stew and realized she had continued adding spice while she talked. "Oops!"

Timothy grimaced. The last time she made chili, it was hot enough to stop one's heart. And the burning that had followed made him wonder if his heart wasn't a bit out of rhythm.

Mother tested some of the concoction and balked. "I can't taste much these days. Can you come tell me if it needs anything?" She spooned some out and held the utensil toward him.

He did not want to be a part of this. But even more he didn't want to hurt her feelings. So, he stepped across the great room. "Just a little. I don't want to spoil my appetite." If he even had one after this.

She pushed the spoon into his mouth.

His breath caught as the overwhelming flavor disappeared in favor of the fire it lit. He coughed.

"Is something the matter?" Her eyes plead, a look of angst on her features.

"No." He slapped his chest and forced himself to swallow. "It's fine."

"You don't think it needs more—?"

"No," the word came out sharper than he'd intended. So he softened his tone. "It's perfect. Just right for a very...unique palate."

She furrowed her brow.

"Trust me, Ma, it's good how it is."

She turned back to her work, and he made his way to the fireside to warm his hands which still chilled despite the intense flame in his throat.

As he settled himself in his father's chair, a knock sounded. Who would be about at this hour? Everyone should be preparing for mealtime. Not making social calls.

Not that he minded delaying his own dinner. For longer than he probably could.

"I'll get it," he called out.

Ma looked at the spice cans as she moved them to the shelf. "Get what?"

He shook his head. This was hopeless. "Someone's at the door."

"Oh," she stared at him. "Then answer it."

His first thought was to tell her that he intended to do just that, but there was no point. "Yes, ma'am."

He resisted leaving the hearth, but he dragged himself to the door and opened it.

Mayor Jacobson stood just outside.

"Mayor! What can I do for you?" Timothy wasn't altogether pleased to see the man. What might he want?

The man took off his hat. "Might I come in?"

Timothy opened the door wider. "Sure."

"What is that...interesting smell?" He glanced toward the kitchen.

"Dinner." Timothy delivered the word without much feeling. The mayor may not approve of his tone, but that man didn't have to eat what Ma had put together.

"Oh. It's quite a...powerful smell."

The mayor was right. It was indeed. Timothy held out a hand toward the dining table. "Care for some coffee?"

Mayor Jacobson appeared as if he considered it but quickly dismissed it. "I can't stay long. I'm sure my own dinner will be waiting on me."

Timothy nodded.

"This isn't cumin." Ma's exasperation was felt even across the house as she looked between two spice tins.

Timothy wanted to agree. But he couldn't bring himself to do it.

"What did she put in it instead?" The mayor's forehead scrunched.

"Sage." There was no need to avoid it. It wasn't as if Ma could hear them over here. "Now, Mayor Jacobson, I'm sure this is not a social call so close to mealtime. What can I do for you?"

The mayor sighed and gripped his hat. "The schoolhouse is badly in need of repairs."

The schoolhouse?

"Apparently, Miss Elston did not keep the town council abreast of certain damages." The mayor did not enjoy this. In fact, he looked downright shamed.

There was no point in this continuing. Timothy hated to turn down the forthcoming offer, but any job with the schoolhouse would involve being around Jane. That was not something he was prepared to do.

"I see. Well, I wish I could help but—"

"Timothy," the mayor cut him off. "I've already spoken with the other men in town that do this kind of work. None are able to commit."

"I'm sorry to hear that, however—"

"The town council is rather eager to have these things addressed. And quickly. We are offering a rather handsome amount. More than the jobs would normally cost. Extra if you can start tomorrow."

Timothy opened his mouth to refuse again but stopped himself. He and his mother were in a desperate situation that would only become all the more dire. And soon. Could he really turn down such a high paying offer?

The mayor seemed to notice the opening Timothy gave him. "If we need to negotiate, there may be a little more we can do."

"Ah, Mayor Jacobson," Ma strolled across the room to greet their guest that she just noticed had entered the home. "I didn't hear you come in."

"Good afternoon to you, Mrs. Johnson. How are you these days?"

"Same as ever. Trying to manage this one." She beamed at Timothy. "He's such a helpful man. And so capable. Just like his Pa, God rest his soul. He'd be right proud of his boy."

Timothy shook off the pang that her words shot through him.

"That he is. Helpful and capable." Mayor Jacobson looked at Timothy. "I can't imagine a more fitting description."

Now the mayor was laying it on thick. Timothy frowned.

"Well, I'll let you two get back to your conversation. I need to get the table set."

Timothy opened his mouth to tell her that he would manage that but didn't have the heart to make her appear less able in front of the mayor. As if the man didn't know already that Ma's health was not what it once was.

"What do you say? Can you *help* us with that building? I won't mince words, it's a big job, but I wouldn't ask if I didn't trust you could do it."

Timothy glared at the man. Enough of this nonsense. Was there really a choice anyway? He tightened his smile and through clenched teeth, said, "All right."

The mayor released an exhale that had him standing more at ease. "I can't tell you how much we appreciate it."

Timothy nodded. "Yes, I'm sure." He ushered the man to the door, ready for his absence.

"You take care, Mrs. Johnson," Mayor Jacobson called in the direction of the table.

"Same to you. Tell your wife I'll see her at the quilting bee on Friday."

"Will do." The mayor set his hat on his head and slipped out of the house.

Timothy was grateful he had left. But his presence...and request... lingered. Yes, Timothy hated his predicament. He would just have to take more care to guard his heart and avoid interacting with Jane. After all, he'd gotten fairly adept at closing off his heart over the last couple of years. He could do it now.

CHAPTER 7

Honesty

Crash!

Jane awoke with a start, jerking up.

It took a few seconds to ground herself. She was in her bedroom at the Sullivan homestead. And she had lain down to rest after getting back.

What was that sound though? High pitched wails came from beyond her door as well. And a burnt smell had eeked into her room. Had something happened?

She slid from the bed, flung the bedroom door open, and rushed to the main living area.

The sight that greeted her stilled her heart. Kitty was on her knees, hunched over. There was broken glass to the right of the dining table, and a pot on the stove produced the overwhelming stench. The shrieking came from Susie and Ellie Mae. Jack held the small girl while trying to console Susie.

Jane moved to Kat, careful to steer around the shards. "What happened?"

She huddled next to Kat. Her friend was shaking uncontrollably. What was going on here?

Jane looked to Jack. "I was by the fireplace with the girls. I'm not sure." His face was strained. For certain, seeing his mother like this had disturbed him. But he was a brave soul, gathering the girls to himself like he did.

"Kat!" Jane raised her voice in hopes that she could snap Kitty out of whatever had taken hold. "Kat, talk to me."

Katherine ignored everything around her, rocking in place, her arms wrapped around herself. At this distance, Jane could see that silent tears streamed down her face.

This wasn't right.

"I'll be right back," Jane told Katherine, though she doubted her friend was aware.

Jane moved to Jack and picked up Susie. "It's all right, sweetheart." She tried to dry the girl's tears. But she wasn't sure she sounded convincing. For certain, she wasn't convinced herself.

"Mama?" the girl sobbed.

"Mama will be fine." Jane prayed that was true. "Jack," she turned to put an arm about his shoulders. "Let's get the girls into Susie's bedroom."

"But, I want to help Ma."

"This is the best thing you can do. I need to get this cleaned up before someone gets hurt." She tossed a long look at her friend, still hunkered and swaying.

"Okay." Jack moved off, with some hesitation, toward the hallway.

"Would you like Jack to play a game with you?" she asked Susie.

The small girl shook her head.

"Come on. Let's be a big brave girl and help Jack take care of Ellie Mae. She might be a little upset."

A puzzled look crossed Susie's face.

"Yes. Babies don't like loud noises. Maybe you and Jack could sing a song to her."

That brought a reaction. Susie's eyes lit up. "Sing to sister?"

"Yes. I think that will be just the thing to calm her down. Can you do that for me?" Jane didn't know how her own voice wasn't shaking. In truth, she was terrified for her friend and these precious children.

They stepped into Susie's room, and Jane set the girl down. "Now, remember what I said. Be brave and help Jack with Ellie Mae."

Susie nodded, though her features belied that she was anything but assured.

Jane looked to Jack. "I'll be back soon." She moved out of the room, careful to close the door. Best to shut the children out from whatever might transpire.

Then she returned to the dining table. Kitty was still just as Jane left her. Should she clean the glass up first? Or tend to Kat?

She bent down beside her friend, "Kat, what's going on? Are you hurt?"

Katherine did not respond, just stared at the glass on the floor. It was eerie.

"I'll take care of that."

Jane went through the motions of cleaning the area, talking with Katherine as she did so, keeping her tone soft and soothing. And she removed the blackened food from the stove. No matter how Jane warred inside with fear, she had to maintain her calm exterior.

After every last shard was picked up, she settled beside Katherine again. "Kat," Jane's voice wavered. No, she could do this. She had to. "I need you to talk to me."

Kitty shook her head. "I...can't do this."

Jane wanted to be confused, but she wasn't. "Do what?"

"All of it." Her voice was quiet. Too quiet. "I...just can't."

Jane wrapped an arm around Katherine's shoulders. "Listen to me. You are the strongest woman I know. Whatever is going on, we can figure it out. We always do."

She pulled Katherine closer. "Now, let me get you resting. I'll manage dinner and the children."

Katherine nodded but didn't say anything. Again, it was unsettling.

Jane worked to help Katherine to her feet and then to her bedroom. Once they were within the darker room, Katherine moved to the bed and curled up on it as if she were a child.

As much as Jane wanted to linger, there were other things—like the children—that needed attention more. Kitty was safe and resting.

Jane checked on Jack and the girls, who were in the midst of singing "Go Tell It On The Mountain." Thank the Lord for Jack, who had the girls giggling. There was still much to do, so she snuck back out of Susie's room.

By the time Wyatt came through the front door, Jane had disposed of the burnt dinner and started roasting some vegetables and chicken.

"Where is everyone?" Wyatt asked as he set his coat on a peg by the door.

"The children are playing in Susie's room and Kitty is lying down."

He nodded. "How are you feeling? Still doing well?"

Jane crossed the kitchen and stopped at the dining table. "I'm well. But..." Why did she hesitate? Expressing her fears to Wyatt was important.

"But what?" His brow furrowed. "Headache?"

"No. It's not me." She took a breath and let it out. "I'm worried about Kat."

Wyatt's features smoothed. And his mouth became a thin line. What did he suspect she would say? Did he already know?

"Let's sit." She indicated the chairs around the table.

But Wyatt stayed as he was, a curious look on his face.

Jane shrugged and pulled out a chair to settle into. "I did try to rest this evening. But I woke up when Kitty broke a lantern. The girls were crying, and I couldn't get Kitty to talk to me."

Wyatt's gaze became dark, but he still wouldn't say anything.

This was difficult. She almost felt as if she were betraying her friend. Though, deep down, she knew she was doing the right thing. "There's something wrong. Kitty is not right."

With slow movements, Wyatt sat and let his weight rest in the chair. He was visibly tense—his shoulders tight and his jaw clenched. "Why would you say that?"

"Have you not seen it? She is tired, emotional, cries a lot, and is troubled...in other ways." Jane couldn't believe Wyatt lacked the observation to have noticed.

"It's normal for a new mother to have crying fits and to be tired." Now it was Wyatt who didn't sound convincing. There was no way he believed that was all.

Jane tried to harden her own features. "You know that's not it."

Wyatt ran a hand through his hair. "What are you saying?"

"I am just not sure that Kitty is herself. And I am worried that things may become less...safe..." Jane swallowed the words that wanted to come. She couldn't make herself say that the children were not safe with Kat. That would be quite the pronouncement over Kat. That didn't make it untrue though.

Wyatt leaned forward on his forearms. "Are you saying she belongs in a sanitarium for her own safety?"

"What? No!" Jane hadn't brought these thoughts to that conclusion. She didn't know what Kitty needed, but she wasn't thinking that. But had Wyatt? Is that why he mentioned it?

"Well, talk like this is exactly the kind of thing that can land someone in one of those places. And I will not do that to her. I can't..." His words caught. "I won't."

Jane's heart went out to him. This was an impossible position he was in. "Maybe there's another option? Something between what it is now and something so extreme."

Wyatt sighed. "I don't know. With my patients, I can't just stay home."

"What about Kitty's mother? Would she be willing to come and stay with her during the day?"

Wyatt nodded. "Possibly."

Jane wondered why he hadn't thought of that already. Or had he? "What is it?"

"I...just didn't want to worry Katie's parents. Especially her mother. Then we'd have two emotionally charged women on our hands."

Jane permitted a smile at his light jest. "Maybe I can tell the mayor that I'm needed here..."

Wyatt shook his head. "No, I need to be honest. With myself and with her parents. It's time I asked for help."

Jane seamed her lips and nodded. She was glad she had prodded him in this direction. But, while they had a possible solution, it didn't fix whatever was going on with Kat. What else could Jane do, though? One thing was certain—she wouldn't give up on her friend.

Timothy gritted his teeth. He'd best go ahead and get this over with. It wasn't as if he could delay. No, Mayor Jacobson and the town council expected him to be at work on these repairs today. He only hoped he was going to the schoolhouse long before Jane would be there.

That was the plan—get there, assess the extent of the damages, make a list, and start work. He hoped he would be able to do the work before and after school only, avoiding Jane as much as humanly possible.

Surely the town council did not expect him to work while school was in session. Even as he pushed on with that assumption, he doubted himself. Mayor Jacobson had been fairly adamant about getting it done quickly. That had been his primary concern.

Timothy shook his head. He would do this his way. It would get done, but he would not risk himself in the process.

He steered the horse past the main stretch in town and to the north toward the schoolhouse. His tools were all in the wagon bed. Perhaps the damage was not as bad as all that and the work would be minor and easy to finish. Then, and only then, might he consider some work during instruction time.

Yes, that would be the best outcome—limited need to be there and less exchange with Jane. It was bad enough that he couldn't keep her out of his thoughts. Or the kiss they had shared.

The schoolhouse sat on the edge of a wooded area, off to the side. Even from here, Timothy could see it needed a fresh coat of paint. That would take time. But was that what the mayor referred to? Surely he wouldn't be so desperate about something that just about any able-bodied man could take care of.

He was relieved to see that the structure appeared to be empty. But was he? There was a discernable droop to his heart. Then he reminded himself that the heart couldn't be trusted. Most assuredly not his.

Bringing the wagon to a halt, he dropped down and tied the horse to the railing.

These steps into the schoolhouse were not in the best shape. He'd hate if one of the children got injured because one of the weakened boards split.

So, new stairs along with the coat of paint.

But as he opened the door, he was hit with a definitely musty odor. What was that coming from?

Sunlight filtered in through the large window in the back of the room. And exposed what exactly he was dealing with.

At first glance, he took in the sizeable hole in the floor and the leaking roof. Was that where the musty smell was coming from? Water seeping in and dousing the floor?

And the room was dreadfully cold. He moved across the space to the wood stove. A quick inspection left him all the more ill. How were these children supposed to learn if they were chilled to the bone? Had Jane attempted to teach under these conditions? How had she fared with the cold air? She was a slight slip of a woman... though there were curves about her.

He slapped the stove. That would not do...neither the lack of proper heat, nor these thoughts. Why couldn't he just let this thing go?

Grimacing, he made a closer inspection of the walls, floor, desks, and everything else in the school room. The reality was not promising. There was extensive work needed. It would take days, weeks, maybe even a month.

He cringed. How did that work out for his carefully laid plans? It did not bode well.

There was chattering of childlike voices outside. He peered out the still open door and noted that the students were arriving. Early?

He tugged out his pocket watch and noted the time. It was nearly time for school to start. Had he lingered so long? And where was Jane?

Did she not make it a point to be here before the children? That was not reassuring.

Should he, then, stay until she did arrive? Perhaps that was best. Not that he wanted to see her, but he didn't want the children to be here unsupervised...especially with these hazardous conditions.

The children appeared surprised to see him. They halted their conversations as they entered and stared as they found their seats.

He nodded and tried to offer them reassuring smiles, but it did not help.

Once the desks were filled, he glanced at his watch again. It was past time for the first lesson to commence. This was even worse—she was late.

But he tried to keep his disappointment in her abilities from his features as he turned toward the students. "Miss Millington is running late today."

And perhaps every day. Maybe this wasn't new to the children. He pushed that thought to the side.

"Let's begin our day with a pledge of allegiance."

The children stood, with some hesitation, and placed hands over their hearts. Then he led them through morning recitations.

And they typically had prayer before school, too, if he remembered correctly. Would he need to see to that? Could he call on one of the students to pray? They all looked at him expectantly.

The back door creaked and opened.

Thank goodness, she had arrived.

But it wasn't Jane that entered, it was Lemuel. How many of the class attendants were late? Jane had set a bad example for them.

Timothy nodded at Lemuel and tried to keep a stern expression from his face. Lemuel likely had a hard enough time getting to school at all with his Pa as he was. There was little room—or reason—for judgment in this case.

"Let's get out your slates and do some calculations." He said the first thing that popped into his head. And hoped that it distracted the children enough from the customary prayer.

The children again paused before obeying. As if he were being strange. Maybe they'd become accustomed to spending the morning as they pleased.

"Um…what math did you work on yesterday?"

There was silence. The students looked at one another, confusion filling the air.

Did Jane not bother with proper instruction either?

"We were adding double digits," an older girl in the front of the room finally answered.

He nodded. At least Jane was doing something.

Making his way to the board, he wrote an addition problem near the top.

Turning back to the students, he was met with puzzled faces. Would the day drag on like this?

The door whooshed open. He wasn't certain if he was more relieved or upset when Jane and Jack appeared. Jane's eyes were red rimmed and her features drawn. What had she been doing that kept her? Clearly, she wasn't well rested.

"You may work in pairs to solve," he said as he moved toward Jane at the back of the room.

As he neared, he ushered Jane back outside. He needed to have a word with her. Now.

Jane didn't know whether to fight Timothy's gentle tug on her arm or lean into him. So clouded was her judgment. And why was he here? Had something happened?

Timothy halted about a yard from the schoolhouse. He folded his arms.

"Would you rather tell the town council that you can no longer teach? Or do I need to tell them about what's going on here?"

"What?" Her reaction was swifter than her thoughts. As she came back around to trying to understand his question, her face heated. "What do you mean 'tell them what's going on here'?"

He let out a breath. "With you."

With her? Because she was late? Is that what he meant? Did he think so little of her?

"I'm afraid I don't understand." She took a step back, needing the distance from him and his angry glare.

"You truly want to do this?" His words were stern. How could he not see that she was already broken down?

"You mean to tell me I should stop teaching because I was late?"

"How are the children supposed to manage themselves with you walking in like this?" He waved a hand at her. "And several minutes late. It may be nothing to you, but I daresay the parents of those children will feel differently."

She drew in a slow breath, trying to steady herself as she did so. "You believe I am perpetually late?"

He raised an eyebrow, but his mouth was still set and firm.

"I'll have you know that I was unavoidably detained this morning." Her voice quivered. Why couldn't she be stronger than this? "And this is the first time I have arrived late. But you wouldn't know that because you aren't here."

He frowned.

"At least...not usually."

"What, pray tell, made you so late today? Something justifiable, I suppose."

Why was he being so hard on her? And why couldn't she calm her racing heart? "As it is, I don't think it's for me to share."

His eyes widened. Did he think she played a game? Or did he realize she referred to Katherine in some way? She couldn't leave breadcrumbs to lead him there.

"That is, I...had challenges that were not simple to solve."

He tightened one side of his mouth as if to smirk.

How dare he. She was worn, weary, and so very distressed. And the person she wanted to turn to more than anyone else had accused her of being negligent. As if that weren't enough, he had all but abandoned her after their shared kiss. Wasn't he, then, the cad?

"Tell the town council if you wish. But I have done nothing wrong."

His face fell then. Did he perhaps know what he had done? How he had injured her heart with his words?

"Jane," he said, his tone softer. "I'm sorry. I shouldn't have—"

"No, you shouldn't have." She crossed her arms, needing more than anything to shield herself. If only she could have guarded her heart better.

Timothy dropped his gaze. "I...don't know what I was thinking."

She seamed her lips. But something nagged at her. Why was he here? Suddenly showing up when she hadn't seen him in days. All that time she had sat in the recovery room, wondering after him...for what? He didn't come. Not once.

"I'd best let you get back to your students."

She nodded, wanting to hold on to her anger. It would be better than feeling the hurt.

He turned and moved off toward his wagon.

And she stepped to the classroom door but halted. She couldn't go on not asking, not knowing. "Timothy..."

He spun, halting his progress. Though he didn't speak, his eyes reflected his sincere regret. Still, it wasn't enough.

She swallowed against a lump in her throat. "Is...is this why you've been avoiding me?" Though something in her knew there must be more to it. But what?

He dipped his head, staring at the ground for a moment.

"See, I...thought," the word caught with emotion. She cleared her throat. "I thought there was...something between us."

He lifted his gaze just enough to look at her. But his features were too obscured for her to get a gauge for what he thought. At length, he shrugged. "I have no good answer. You didn't deserve that."

She gripped her shaking hands together in hopes that it would still them. And though she waited for him to say more, he didn't.

The door creaked behind her, and she spotted several sets of eyes staring out. How long had the eavesdroppers been listening?

"I have to get back to my class."

He nodded but didn't move.

Why did she want things to be all right between them? She didn't need this hurt. Perhaps she'd do better to protect herself from this in the future.

Jane turned and slipped back into the classroom, shooing the students back to their desks. And she bit her lip as she reminded herself where she was and why she was here. She couldn't let Timothy affect her like this. Not now. Not ever again.

CHAPTER 8

Closer

Timothy pulled his horse and wagon to a stop at the school. Yet again.

He had been at this building too much in the last few days. It didn't help that he focused his time on the off hours. Still, it had to be done. And he brought fresh boards to finally repair the hole in the floor.

Dropping out of the wagon, he tied the horse's reins to the railing and grabbed for his boards.

But as he pushed the door open, he noticed Jane was still within.

He halted, unsure of how to proceed.

Her gaze caught his.

"I...didn't know you would still be here. I don't want to disturb your—"

She waved him off. "Don't worry about it. Feel free to do what you need to."

He hesitated but knew it was for the best he get after that hole. It was a miracle that none of the children had been injured already. "I'll try to keep it quiet."

Was that a promise he could really keep? Hammering boards into place, ripping out the damaged section...it wasn't quiet work.

"Don't mind me." She didn't look up from her papers as she said it.

What was she working on, after all? Lesson preparations? Grading work? Why didn't she go back to the Sullivan homestead for that? Such was none of his business.

So, he moved across the room to the gaping section in the floor.

He was glad that Jane had kept the wood stove going. There was still a chill in the air outside. It was for her comfort...well, and the comfort of the students that he had attended to those repairs first.

Perhaps he shouldn't, but he looked toward her, huddled over the large desk, with only a light shawl about her shoulders. That was his doing. He had added to her comfort. That meant something to him. Did it mean something to her?

He grimaced at that thought. After the way he had talked to her, judged her...he wouldn't blame her if she never forgave him. He'd been just awful.

Resisting the urge to hang his head, he refocused on the work before him. The pieces of wood around the gap had been cracked and splintered. He would need to cut back a portion of them to make more secure spaces for the new boards.

Tossing another look at Jane, he watched as she lit a lantern near her desk.

Was she planning to be here much longer? Had his presence not made her wish for escape? It was not much, but it was something.

As he worked, he couldn't shake the feel of her presence nearby. Not even as he tried to home in on his work. She was quiet. Not normal for her more outgoing personality. But he couldn't blame her. He had shattered what trust existed between them. And any goodwill she might have for him. Her worst would be no less than he deserved.

He tried to work the last board loose. It gave way only for a deep sting to overtake him. Had he injured his hand? The pain radiated from the palm of his right hand. Pulling the injured limb to himself, he discovered a shard of wood buried in his skin.

Could he not avoid injury any better than this? First his thumb, then his hand. Was he so driven to distraction?

"What is it?"

He jerked his regard in Jane's direction as her concerned words fell on him.

She had stood and now watched him intently.

"It's nothing," he said, attempting to push words through clenched teeth without seething.

"I dare say it is not." Her footfalls neared.

How did he get himself in these predicaments? What could he do? He wanted to push back and hope she would return to her work. But he knew better. Though he had been terrible toward her, though his every word to her merited an uncaring response…that was not who she was.

He rose from the floor. Had he fallen over when the board broke loose?

"Let me see," she said, her words kind. More so than he ever thought to have directed at him again.

"It does not warrant disrupting your work." He held his hand close to his body. It certainly did smart. But that didn't mean she needed to worry after it.

She held out her hands. "Just let me see it."

How was she so considerate after what he had said and done? But her warmth tugged at him. Her eyes called to him. He was helpless to refuse her, so he set his hand in hers.

She leaned closer to his palm, examining the wound.

But all he could think about was the scent of gardenias coming from her. And how intoxicating the warmth pooling in his stomach was at her nearness.

"I think I can get this out." She blew out a breath and met his gaze. "It may hurt. The splinter is rather large."

He lost his ability to speak, so taken with her. His mind filled with what a pleasing thing it would be to pull her to himself and taste her lips once more.

"You all right?" The concern in her voice had deepened.

He nodded but could not take his eyes off her as she bent back over his hand. And though his hand pinched at her ministrations, he found he didn't mind it one bit. Her breathing filled his senses, and he wondered if she could hear his heart beating.

She shot a look in his direction. "I'm sorry." Then she looked to his hand again.

Those were words she certainly didn't owe him. Rather, he should have spoken them to her a dozen times over for his behavior. For his quick judgment of her.

The pinch became a burn, and then there was relief.

"Done." There was something victorious in the word she spoke over him.

His heart dropped. Now she wouldn't need to be so near him. This heat between them would dissipate in the distance created. How would he stand it?

He gripped her hand.

She looked at the fingers clamped over hers and then her gaze rested on him, a question in her eyes. A curiosity mixed with anguish. Did she still hurt so from his cowardly words?

"Jane, I..."

She blinked several times. To keep her emotions at bay?

He stepped closer. There was now not much space between them.

She mumbled. But he couldn't hear it over the pounding in his ears.

"Hmmm?" he murmured.

"Can...can I ask you something?" Her voice was light and airy. Almost breathless. Dare he hope that she would be swept into this intense moment with him?

"Anything." The word came unbidden. He shouldn't say such, but everything in him wanted to absolve himself of this guilt, this ache, and, more than that, give him permission to...what? Touch her? Be close to her?

"What...what happened between you and Kat?"

Jane hesitated, then found the courage to lift her gaze to Timothy's eyes once more.

He was difficult to read, mouth a thin line and eyes fathomlessly deep. What was she thinking? He either just didn't want to share or just plain wanted to leave without upsetting her again. Here he was, seeking friendship, and she had taken it a step too far.

She looked away. "I'm sorry." The words were choked out. Her emotions were running away with her better judgment. "I shouldn't have asked. None of this is my business." Turning to move away, she swallowed back a lump in her throat.

He caught her arm, halting her progress.

She jerked her regard to him.

His face was still an unreadable mask. "It's not that." He loosened his hold and slid hands up her arms to hold her elbows.

She responded to his unspoken request, resting her hands on his forearms.

"It's just...difficult for me to think about it. Much less talk about it."

She shook her head while looking down. "You don't have to, I—"

"I want to." He tipped her face upward with a crooked finger on her chin. His eyes had brightened with a sincerity she had not known from him.

She swallowed again. This time because she felt the air in the room had thinned. Or something was causing her light-headedness.

"Katie and I..." He cleared his throat. "Katherine and I grew up together. That much you probably know."

Jane nodded.

"I guess I always thought of her. And hoped."

Something about that statement made Jane's heart drop.

"When she returned from San Francisco, we courted." He paused then.

Was it because there were harder things to share? Or because he changed his mind about sharing it? Jane prayed he would find it in himself to be open. That there was hope here where only faith had been.

"And...when the children needed a family, she asked if I was ready to get married and help provide that home."

Jane wanted to look away so he wouldn't see the disappointment that must be shining through her eyes. But his gentle grip on her chin prevented it.

"I wasn't ready. I...thought it wasn't the right reason to take that next step. And so, she married Wyatt."

His jaw clenched so hard she saw the muscles twitch.

"Do you...regret it? Not accepting her offer?"

His brows furrowed.

Jane feared the worst. Was he still in love with her friend? That would certainly explain things.

Timothy's gaze traveled over her features. "I did for a long time. I couldn't seem to get away from the loss. I...even left the ministry."

"You were a preacher?" Her words were gentle, though she had no doubt her voice was laced with surprise.

He nodded. "Yes. For many years, I was the preacher here in Cripple Creek. After Katherine and Wyatt married, I...just couldn't stay. But the shadows of what happened followed me even to my next post. And I couldn't make sense of God in that place. So, I gave it up."

His tone made it as if it were simply that. But she saw in his eyes that it was more. Much more.

She lifted a hand and brushed fingers against the side of his face. "I'm sorry...that it happened. You must care for her a great deal."

He watched her expression. What else could he see?

"And that it took you from your calling."

He shrugged. "Perhaps it never should have been my calling."

She frowned. And wondered why God had, to some extent, allowed such hardship on one of His more loyal servants.

Her fingers still grazed his cheek. She pulled her hand back. "I think I am still looking for my calling." The words were out before she could stop them. Did she really feel that way?

"What about teaching?"

"It was a means to an end. I had to get out of my aunt's home and find a way to support myself. There aren't many...virtuous occupations for women."

He grimaced.

"Yes. Besides, my aunt was insistent that I couldn't...and shouldn't...ever rely on a man to solidify my future."

That brought on a strange look from him. Brow creased and mouth downturned. "What about your parents?" He said it as if he already knew.

"They died when I was young. My aunt raised me."

His frown deepened. "I'm so sorry."

She shrugged. She did not want his pity. "I was fortunate to have family to take me in. There are many who end up in terrible situations after being orphaned."

His eyes glistened as he met her gaze. There was a softness to his regard. And a warmth. She wished she could wrap herself in it, ward off the chill of the evening...and of the hard realities of life.

His hand on her chin slid to her jawline. "That doesn't mean you had it easy."

She looked down.

He spread his thumb and fingers apart to tip her head back just so. Then she delved into his eyes again. There was something more there than she had noticed before. And the space between their bodies seemed to heat several degrees.

His gaze flicked to her lips, and she wondered if he was only tempted because of their closeness or if he felt drawn because of this thing growing between them.

Then he leaned in and pressed his lips to hers.

The kiss was very different than the contact they had shared before. That had been tentative and curious. This was slow, tender, and full of promise. A promise, she prayed he could keep.

Timothy tasted her lips, savoring each contact as if it would be the last. But it felt more like a beginning, with all the hope in the world. He became lost in this shared moment.

Jane leaned into him, a soft sound coming from her throat. Indeed, their kiss seemed to affect her as much as it did him.

He wrapped his arms more tightly around her, pressing more deeply into her, wishing he could melt into her as much as she had him.

Their kisses became more fervored, more hungry. He wanted more. But dare he push further?

She was innocent and pure...and he was risking her reputation as it was.

Though everything in him screamed for him not to do so, he pulled his mouth from hers.

A small sound of protest fell from her lips. And she clung to him as if she would lose her balance otherwise. He, too, felt his whole body sway, as their contact had his head swimming.

She settled her head into the place where his neck met his shoulder. And sighed.

He tucked her there, kissing her hair and breathing in the floral scent of it.

Jane continued to lean on him, and he relished it—the feeling of her and the reality of her trust in him. He would not betray it by taking liberties not due him.

Timothy became more aware of what their situation had become —they were alone, and the daylight had given way to darkness. The lantern now provided the only light in the room.

It shone on her hair, bringing out the many golden tones there. She was perfect. But it couldn't last. At least not tonight.

"I'd best get you back to the homestead." It was a difficult thing to force out. Would it be even more difficult to do?

She muttered, "All right." There was a tinge of sadness to her voice as if his declaration had stifled what had happened between them.

He leaned back just far enough that he could look down at her. "Hey," he said as he stroked her hair and back. "It's for the best. I do not want to damage your reputation."

"Oh." Her reply lilted upward as if that had not occurred to her. Yes, she was innocent indeed.

With a great measure of effort, he withdrew his arms and set her back from him as far as he could withstand. Which was not quite an arm's length.

"Let me escort you so you can get some rest."

She looked at the desk, papers still strewn about. "But—"

"I don't think either of us will be effective at this hour." He smiled.

She nodded, her lips tugging upward.

Why did he have to focus on them? They drew him to reclaim that intimacy they had shared.

He took her hand and placed it in the crook of his elbow. "Shall we?"

She tossed one last look at the desk before gazing up at him. "Very well."

He touched her cheek. "It will keep. I promise."

Her eyes closed at his touch.

There was much reason to be mindful and careful with her... both with the exchanges they had made here, and with her heart.

Timothy bent down to get the shawl that had dropped at some point. He wrapped it around her shoulders and led her out to the cart.

After settling her there, he excused himself to quickly arrange his tools and the board pieces to the side so they wouldn't cause an accident for any children coming into the schoolhouse.

Then he rushed back outside. She watched the door, waiting for him. His heart fluttered. Did she truly care as much as she seemed to? Could he really handle that?

He pushed that question to the side for another time. And smiled at her before untying the reins and climbing up to the driver's box.

She wrapped her arms around his closest to her and leaned against him. Because of the chill? Or to further their connection?

He hoped he wasn't alone in that desire.

As he steered the horse and cart along, he set a hand to hers and squeezed. That was all he could offer before turning his attention back to directing the animal. If he could tear his mind from her at all.

The appearance of the Sullivan home in the distance came too soon. Despite his best intentions to keep some distance for his heart's sake, he began to realize it was for naught. For he couldn't give himself to this thing between them and still protect his heart.

Now just beyond the porch steps, he turned to her. "Thank you. For listening."

She nodded. "Thank you for...sharing."

Their breaths mingled and he found it impossible to maintain even this distance. He slanted his mouth over hers once more for a kiss as tender as he could manage.

Her hand cupped the side of his face and he wanted to pull her to his chest.

"Jane, is that..." a voice off to the left called before trailing.

Too late, Timothy realized the door had creaked open. He pulled back to find Katherine watching them.

CHAPTER 9

Fallout

J ane felt Timothy's muscles tense. His arms tightened even as they released her. What was going through his mind?

Kitty stared, mouth agape. Was it so bad? Should Jane feel guilty?

"Kat, I..." But Jane couldn't think of what to say next. What was there to say?

The front door opened wider, and Wyatt walked out. "What's going on out here?" He paused as he, too, set eyes on Jane and Timothy. Were they too close to each other? Did he know what had transpired?

An awkwardness filled the space, even as great as it was, between all parties. Jane wasn't sure what she should say, but the nervousness radiating off Timothy pressed her to speak.

Before she could, however, Wyatt wrapped an arm around Kitty's shoulders. "Let's get you back inside." He tossed Jane and Timothy another disapproving look before ushering Kitty within.

Timothy let out a breath, but it did nothing to ease his tension.

Would he say something? Jane desperately wanted him to. For she had no gauge of how he felt, other than his tension. Was he embarrassed? Did he regret their kiss? More and more his reaction gave Jane reason to wonder if he was, in fact, still in love with her friend.

This weighed her chest down. Could she push through that?

She set a tentative hand on Timothy's shoulder. "I'll talk to Kat." Though it was the last thing she wanted to do, it was best. To preserve both relationships—hers and Kitty's as well as hers and Timothy's.

Losing either one would devastate her at this point. For hope had blossomed within her. Might Timothy be her place to belong?

No longer able to sit in the tense moment, she moved to climb down.

"Let me help you." Timothy finally spoke. But his words were plain and difficult to feel out what he thought.

He dropped down and came around. Even as he set hands to Jane's waist, his touch was stiff. There was no hint of the tenderness he had just had for her.

That did not help the situation. But what could she expect from him?

As she attained a firm footing, she was loath to release Timothy's shoulders. Couldn't he give her a sign—a look, a touch, a word—that reflected what had happened between them? Or was she expecting too much from the moment?

His hands did not linger about her waist. He pulled back, and a thick awkwardness filled that space.

She looked up into his eyes, but his gaze darted to the left. Why wouldn't he even look at her? "Timothy, I don't want—"

"It's late," he said flatly.

Words at last! But not what she had hoped for.

Perhaps she should not wish for more. This had to be difficult for him.

So, she reached up to graze the side of his face. Just because he wouldn't express his heart didn't mean she couldn't reassure him of her feelings, did it?

He touched her wrist but let it slide from his grasp.

She looked down. "I'd best get inside."

He nodded.

Then she pulled back and walked up the stairs to the porch.

She felt Timothy's eyes on her, but he didn't say another word.

Jane offered him another glance as she reached for the door's latch. Then she pushed within and shut the door, barring her from more distress at Timothy's reluctance.

She wanted to lean back against the door and...what? Pray? Bemoan her luck? Be thankful for Timothy's openness...and his expression of his feelings in the way he had kissed her?

But as she closed the door, she found herself facing a bewildered Kitty and a less-than-pleased Wyatt.

She let out a long sigh. This would not be pleasant.

"Are you all right?" Wyatt's words were gentle despite the hardness of his features.

"Of course." What could he mean? Did he think Timothy attacked her? If that were the case, why did Wyatt not step in sooner?

Jane moved closer to where they sat at the dining table, holding hands. Wyatt also moved a hand up and down Kitty's arm. To soothe her? Did she, too, still have a care for Timothy?

"Kat..." Jane started, unsure of how to proceed.

Kitty blinked.

"Are you all right?" Jane homed in on her friend's reaction, trying to ignore Wyatt's frown.

Kitty nodded. But her eyes told a different story. Was this a product of her recent emotional challenges? Or had she been so disturbed by seeing Jane and Timothy's interaction?

Wyatt leaned closer to Kat. "It's probably time you got some rest." Then he looked at Jane. "We can talk more in the morning."

Was the strain of the moment too much to put on Kat? Jane worried that it might be. So, she only watched as Wyatt led Kitty to the hallway. "I'll be there in a minute."

Kitty only nodded as she walked into their bedroom.

Wyatt turned back to Jane. What did he want?

"Be careful." His words were not harsh or judgmental. But filled with concern. Should she be more apprehensive about Timothy? Was there something she didn't know?

Her heart ached at the way her dear friends reacted. After a kiss that had flown her to the stars, the crash back to reality was hard.

Wyatt shifted back to his and Kitty's bedroom. And disappeared.

Jane sank into the closest chair. What would tomorrow bring?

Timothy closed the barn door after putting his horse away for the night. What an evening this had been. An unexpected evening at that. Being found out by Katie had left him muddling in confusion. But he wasn't sure he wished he hadn't kissed Jane. If he were to pursue Jane, then he would have to come to grips with Katie knowing at some point. Why not now?

He did regret parting with Jane the way he had. Though much of his reaction had been just that—a reaction. Especially when Wyatt showed up. That had sealed his fate, at least on his ability to control his emotions. The remainder of his time there had been strained.

What must Jane think? Perhaps he would have to go to the school even earlier tomorrow. Then he may be able to steal some moments to apologize. Her consideration and willingness to hear him out earlier had endeared her to him. She was kind and considerate. And though she had sought answers, she hadn't pushed for them.

The question remained: what was he going to do about it?

With the kisses they shared, it seemed he had already decided. He cared for her. Wanted to spend more time with her. Court her.

Most assuredly he did.

He couldn't let Katherine and Wyatt interfere and destroy his chance for happiness. Having done that once in his lifetime was far and beyond enough.

Stepping into the house, he spotted his mother in the chair by the fire.

"You're still awake, Ma?" he called.

No response.

She must have fallen asleep reading. It happened often.

He moved about the kitchen, trying to find something to eat. The woman had already cleaned after the dinner meal. But she usually left him a...

Then he spotted the plate on the dining table. He removed the covering. Pot roast. Moving the plate close to his face, he breathed in the aroma of the savory beef and vegetables.

Though it did not erase his memory of the scent of gardenias that had filled his senses for most of the evening.

Even though he was much distracted, he silently thanked his mother for her thoughtfulness.

He glanced over in her direction. Indeed, her head rested against the back of the chair, a Bible open on her lap.

As much as Timothy wanted to cringe at it, he couldn't. His mother loved God yet had shown him understanding and grace when he left the pulpit for good. Though he knew it had to have bothered her...at least a little. She had never spoken to that affect.

He took a bite of potato. It was a bit bland...and cold. Ma seemed to be having a more difficult time lately with her mind. She read things a bit oddly and her cooking just wasn't right. How else had she been affected?

Perhaps he should swallow his pride and speak with Wyatt about it.

But the idea of facing Wyatt anytime in the near future brought a cold sweat to his face. It wasn't as if Wyatt was Jane's father. Or caretaker. What was it to Wyatt if Timothy courted her?

Indeed, who should he ask? She mentioned she was raised by a spinster aunt. And that she now lived in a boarding house alone. Perhaps the last of her relatives had passed.

He finished his dinner and set the plate by the wash bin. Now he would have to wake Ma and get her to bed. Not something he wanted to do. More and more she was difficult to rouse with her hearing all but gone. And she slept dreadfully soundly.

But she would be more comfortable in her bed, he was quite certain.

Walking toward the dying fire, he glanced at her. Though the cabin was dim, he could make out her peaceful form.

He stoked the fire a bit, but not too much. For he planned to get some sleep himself soon.

Glancing at the open Bible in her lap, he noted the passage: Zephaniah 3. A promise for the Israelites, that they would return after their exile. He frowned.

It wasn't his favorite part of Scripture. But he related more now than ever...feeling like a bit of an exile himself. It seemed God was farther away than ever. Did He care about Timothy's pain? Did He see? Regardless of what Scripture promised, Timothy felt alone.

It was best he press those thoughts and questions to another time. He was weary—emotionally and physically. The night had been a long one already. Though he was certain it would turn out to be too short for adequate rest.

"Ma," he yelled in her direction.

No reaction. One of those nights...where she slept hard.

But something nagged at him.

"Ma," he stepped closer.

Her features had lost quite a bit of color. Was she ill?

He reached out to touch her shoulder. Still no response.

Something wasn't right here.

He examined her face now that he was closer. Her skin was ashen and her lips almost a purple color.

"No," he whispered the word out loud. Then he fell to his knees, unable to stand any longer.

His mother had passed into eternity.

Jane hesitated at the door to her bedroom. She heard the sounds of activity in the great room and beyond. Were Wyatt and Kitty up? What would she say to them? How could she calm this situation while being true to her heart?

Hiding would get her nowhere. She drew in a breath and pressed the door open.

Sure enough, there were words passing between Wyatt and Jack. Maybe no one else was about. Not that she looked forward to that look of disappointment being repeated on Wyatt's face.

She reminded herself that she shouldn't care. And stepped into the great room.

Wyatt stopped talking mid-sentence. He worked with a skillet by the stovetop. The smell of bacon and eggs had filled the room.

"Pa?" Jack said as he set a cup of water on the table.

"Yes, Jack, go ahead and get your sister up and ready, if you will. I don't want Grandma to have to worry with that."

Jack nodded, tossed a look at Jane and smiled, then moved off down the hall.

Leaving her and Wyatt in awkward silence.

"Good morning," Jane offered as she moved to the cabinet. Should she just act as if nothing happened? That would be preferable, but she was not that naïve. That would not go over well.

"Morning," Wyatt said, turning his attention back to the food.

"May I?" She moved closer to the stove with her mug and reached for the coffee pot.

"Of course." Wyatt shifted a bit so she could reach it.

She filled her mug and sipped it, though it was quite hot and rather strong, as usual.

"Hey," Wyatt said as he shot a glance down the hall. To ensure the children couldn't hear? What was she in for? "I'm sorry about the way things went last night."

That surprised her. "Oh?"

"Yes. Katie and I felt bad that we reacted so...badly."

Jane stared at him. All her trepidation had been for naught. Everything would be fine.

"It's just…" he started.

Here it comes.

"We just worry about you. We want the best for you."

"And you're certain that's not Timothy?" she challenged.

Wyatt grimaced as if her words hurt. "That's not up to us."

Jane let out the air pent up in her chest and eased her shoulders. *Relax.* He was being reasonable.

"We just…have had some experiences with Timothy that aren't very…positive."

"Yes, he told me that you two eloped while he and Kitty were courting."

Wyatt's eyes widened, and he looked stunned. "He told you that?"

"Yes." Jane squared her shoulders. This may not go so poorly after all.

"Did he also tell you that he made an overture toward Katie *after* she and I were man and wife? That he believed our marriage would be annulled and felt it was up to him to help her see that?"

Jane's shoulders fell. "No."

Wyatt faced Jane, setting the food that smelled as if it had started to burn, to the side of the stove, off the heat. "There are…two sides to every story. But I warn you, Timothy did not play the part of the upstanding friend and certainly didn't uphold his image as a man of the cloth either."

"And you judge him for that?" It was a statement more than a question.

Wyatt frowned. "We are just cautious. And it would be best for you to be as well."

Jane nodded. Guilt for thinking worse of Wyatt shadowed her thoughts. He and Kitty really did just care about her.

"I appreciate your concern. But I think Timothy has changed."

Wyatt shrugged and let out a sigh. "I hope so."

The door to a bedroom down the hall shut, and Jack and Susie emerged.

"Bacon?" The little girl's eyes lit up as she asked.

Wyatt scooped her up. "Yes, Susie-girl, we are having bacon, but you have to eat your eggs, too."

The small child's face scrunched, and her nose wrinkled.

"Deal?" Wyatt put out his free hand.

Her features smoothed and she shook his hand. "Deal."

Jack pulled out the chair Jane normally sat in.

She thanked him and lowered into it. Then she thought better of it and twisted toward Wyatt. "Did you need any help?"

"Nope. It's about done. Hope you're hungry." He beamed at her.

She was relieved that things were settling now that he had said his piece. "I am."

As the rest of the family took their seats, Jane stared at Kitty's place. Would she sleep through breakfast again? Of late, she stayed abed until after Jane had left for school. Jane wasn't actually sure when Kitty would get out of bed. Perhaps long after Wyatt left everything in Lauren Matthew's capable hands.

Wyatt seemed to notice her staring. "Katie is...getting some extra sleep. She was rather tired."

Jane knew it was a cover up. Wyatt had switched Ellie Mae to bottles so that Kitty didn't have to get up in the night. Though she spent more time in bed these days. Frowning, Jane held out her plate. She would not bare her concerns in front of the children. The less they knew, the better.

But as she looked at Jack, she spotted the same longing in his regard as he stared at his mother's chair.

This was all so much more complicated than just what went on between her and Timothy. Would this home ever be right again?

CHAPTER 10

Grief

Dawn pressed in on Timothy. Had the sun risen? Was it day? Somehow, he had drifted to sleep at last. For now, he opened his eyes after the long, dark night and saw light.

He was still sitting in Pa's chair, holding his mother's last crochet project—a blanket for who knows who. That was not something he had bothered to ask. There were a lot of things he had not bothered to ask.

Rising, he found his muscles had cinched in the uncomfortable position he had kept himself in. What had awakened him? For he was no less tired. It had been a rather long night with the undertaker. Now there was nothing to keep him from his rest except...

Knock, knock, knock.

He turned toward the front door. Was someone here? Who would come at such an ungodly hour? And just after his mother had...?

It just didn't seem right. But maybe his mother had made plans with someone. Or one of her friends stopped by to see her. Could he handle having to share the news of Ma's passing? He doubted it, but he also didn't know how to avoid it.

He moved to the door and opened it.

Reverend Dawson stood on the front porch.

Not him. Not now.

But Timothy couldn't make himself send the man away. The preacher only did as he must. As much as Timothy didn't want to discuss these things, it had to be. Now or later. Perhaps best now.

"Come in, Reverend." Timothy moved back from the door, wishing his legs weren't so sluggish.

The older man entered and shut the door. "I'm so sorry to hear about your mother."

Of course, he was. Whether he really was or not. Timothy had been through this very conversation, from Reverend Dawson's end, so many times. How could he expect any different from this man?

"Can I get you anything?" Timothy must play his part, too. "Coffee? Tea? Anything?"

The man hesitated as if he weren't certain. Timothy could likely recite what went through the reverend's thoughts: How long would this take? Would the grieving family member be more open if they chatted over a hot mug of some sort?

"I thank you, I'd like some coffee, please."

So, he had decided Timothy was that kind of parishioner. One who needed to be coddled a bit.

It shouldn't bother him, but something about it stung.

"Make yourself at home." Timothy moved toward the kitchen.

He started the coffee pot and waited, not caring where the reverend sat or what he thought. Timothy could not help but imagine his mother in this space. Most of his life, she spent in here— baking, cooking, preparing something for someone. Always about others, never about her.

Reverend Dawson remained quiet as Timothy prepared the two steaming mugs and brought them to the table.

Only then did he notice that the preacher had been perusing the living space, looking at this and that. Perhaps gathering thoughts for the eulogy. Not that it mattered to Timothy. It was just a bit odd to be on this side of the situation.

The reverend joined him at the table, smiling ever so slightly as he pulled one mug toward himself. "Thank you."

Timothy waved off the comment. He didn't need it. There were social niceties and Timothy could manage those by himself.

At least that.

But as he settled into his seat, there was an awkwardness that developed. Reverend Dawson was not much of a talker. Certainly not chitchat kind of talking.

"I...um..." The preacher coughed before continuing, "I see you haven't put the family photographs down." He indicated the photo of Timothy's father and the one of the whole family unit on the mantel.

Timothy's gaze landed on the old, worn photographs. "Oh. I don't give much credence to such superstitions."

"Others will. It might be best to put them down or away entirely before the wake starts." The man's bushy eyebrows drew upward.

Timothy shook his head. Such nonsense was the last thing he wanted to deal with right now.

"I understand that some of the church ladies will be here to help lay her out." Reverend Dawson took a long sip. "Or have they already come?" He glanced about the great room.

"No. No one has been here yet. Except the undertaker, that is."

The reverend leaned forward, and his voice took on a gentle quality. "I know this is all very difficult, Mr. Johnson. Please let us know whatever the church can do to help you."

Timothy couldn't look at the preacher. Who could help him, truly? He was alone in the world. Completely. Alone.

"I don't have to tell you how much the people of this town love and respect you. And your mother."

No. He didn't. Although Timothy would trade it all for one more moment to ask his mother what to do now. How could he be at such a loss? Everything had been planned, perfectly. Then, since Wyatt and Katie's betrayal, his life had been in a tailspin.

But what of Jane? Something in his mind whispered, urging him to think about her. He had done enough of that as it was. Where were things with Jane? What did he want? Could he drag her into his grief? No. This was his burden. And he would bear it alone.

Perhaps it would be best if he mustered through these traditions and got back to his life—what there was of it—and forget these distractions.

"Mr. Johnson?"

The words pulled him out of his thoughts.

Reverend Dawson was staring at him.

"Yes? Oh, sorry, Reverend, I was...well, I was distracted."

The older man nodded. "It is to be expected. But I wondered if we might arrange to talk soon about the burial."

Why did the man feel the need to rush things? Was this how all the loved ones Timothy visited after a death felt? Crowded, suffocated, wanting to be left alone?

"I can see your mind is much elsewhere. But I want you to know that you are surrounded by friends."

Timothy stared blankly at the man. "What?"

"The townspeople...we are your friends and want to support you. You don't have to do this alone."

"Except that I do."

The preacher jerked back.

"I know all the ins and outs of talking with bereaved family and friends. There's nothing you can say that I haven't said a hundred times over. So, you can save your breath."

Why was he being so ridiculous? Lashing out at the man who just wanted to fulfill his duty? Well, Timothy didn't care. He wasn't just another townsperson. His mother wasn't. She had been a rock for this community. And...and...

He shook his head and cleared his throat against the forming lump as he stood. "I have to get ready for the wake. You'll have to excuse me."

Reverend Dawson rose as well. "I...thank you for the coffee." He didn't seem to know what else to say.

Timothy wasted no time in crossing to the door and opening it, the preacher fast on his heels. As if even he wanted to quit the place as quickly as possible.

Once the man was out of Timothy's home, he shut the door. And leaned against it. Nothing would ever be the same again. And no one could do anything about it.

The school day came to a close, and Jane watched the last of the children rush off—to home, to their loved ones. What waited for her back at the homestead was...less comforting.

Kitty had continued to struggle. It was impossibly difficult for Jane to watch. Wyatt had been so strong. Every step of the way. But what went on in his mind? Was he as assured as he appeared?

Jane had reason to doubt.

As she stepped back into the building, her gaze flitted over the tools Timothy had left behind. He had not bothered them since the previous night when they had...shared a moment. Why hadn't he come today? Was he ashamed? Did he regret their connection?

Her face flushed as she remembered how she had clung to him. Maybe it hadn't been what he wanted at all. And she had thrown herself at him.

The tightness in her chest would not let up. She couldn't think about that. What's done...is done. And she couldn't change it. But what did she want? For him to court her? Give her some reason to hope for better things in the future? A family? A place to belong?

Or was she simply a foolish girl...wishing for things that would always be denied her?

Frank had certainly felt that there was no place for her in his world after she told him about...

She shook her head. No point in dwelling on the past.

Turning back to the desk, she made short work of closing everything up for the day. Even if she wanted to, she couldn't stand to linger here...questioning and guessing what might have happened to keep Timothy away.

Or would he come in time? If she waited, would he show up, hoping to have avoided her?

She would not give him the satisfaction of finding her waiting. Resigned, she stepped out and closed the door. Solidly.

The walk to the General Store was short but lengthened by her pondering. And loneliness. She slipped within, hoping to find distraction aplenty.

A couple of women chatted near the ribbon. Perhaps Jane might grab that last. She also needed some apples for a pie. Just because she was alone, didn't mean she couldn't treat Kitty and Wyatt to some good food.

She maneuvered around the women, excusing herself as she did so, and moved toward the barrels.

"The poor thing," one of the women said, clucking her tongue. "Wonder what he'll do now."

"Hard to say," the other chimed in. "He used to be such a solid man. Dependable. But these days, who knows?"

Jane didn't intend to overhear, but there was little else to do as she searched out a few good apples.

"His mother was the only thing holding him here, I suppose."

"Whatever will he do to support himself if he moves off? Though, his load is lightened a bit."

"If you can call it that. Mrs. Johnson really did take care of him."

"He's a fine man. I am surprised he hasn't settled down."

"After that business with the doctor's wife, I can't blame him for being a bit gun shy."

Wait...were they talking about...Timothy? Now she shifted to hear better.

"I'm not even sure I know what ever happened. Was she ill?"

"Not that I'm aware of. He apparently just came home last night and found her. That's what the undertaker said."

Undertaker? Did something happen to Timothy's mother? She could hardly breathe. Dare she interrupt the women? They had started to move off.

She needed to find Timothy. Now.

Setting the apples down, she raced to the livery, probably to the further speculation of those women. But she cared not. Timothy might need her. And nothing would stop her.

The banging at the door shook Timothy from his sleep. Not again. Would he be visited by Reverend Dawson a second time today? How was he to tolerate it? Perhaps he could just send the man away.

Whether he should or not, that was his plan.

He crossed the room and opened the door.

Four very sorrowful older women were on his front porch. Oh yes, the preacher had mentioned they would come.

He frowned. This would not be pleasant. Couldn't he just be left alone? After all, that's what he was, wasn't he? Alone. Nowhere to belong.

Pressing a small smile onto his features, he swung the door wider. "Thank you for coming." The words felt forced, did they sound that way?

The women seemed not to mind. One of the women to the right leaned forward. "We're so sorry, Rev— Mr. Johnson. What a rough thing to be going through."

He nodded. Did they truly understand though? Surely at their age, they had lost parents. But they were also likely married and settled by that time. Not him.

"Please, come in." Another thing he didn't mean. Would this day of faked pleasantries ever end?

Mrs. Jacobson, who was the only one of the group who had retained some brown about her hair, spoke up. "Let me make you a cup of coffee."

"That's not necessary."

Another woman—Mrs. Batson—patted his hand. "It is our pleasure to help you." Then she nodded at Mrs. Jacobson, who shuffled off into the kitchen.

He shrugged but tried to downplay how put out he was in the moment.

Mrs. Batson's eyes darted about the large space. "Where is she?"

Confusion swept him for a moment. "Oh. Her bedroom."

The remaining two women moved around Mrs. Batson and him toward the back rooms.

"Now..." Mrs. Batson glanced about the space. "Let's see what else needs to be tended to."

"I can manage all right, I—"

She set a hand to his arm. "Ruth was our dear friend. Let us honor her this way. The same as she would have for any one of us."

He nodded as Mrs. Batson passed him and moved about the great room. She set the pictures face down on the mantel.

"Actually, I..." Timothy spoke up. How was he to express to the woman that he cared not to cater to such ideas? He certainly didn't believe that any of the people in the pictures would be possessed by his mother's spirit. Such thoughts.

The woman turned.

"I..." He cleared his throat. "I would rather keep those up."

Mrs. Batson's eyes widened. And she stepped to him. "It is what is expected."

"That doesn't mean I want to participate." He kept his voice calm, but a storm raged in him. How was this honoring his mother? To play into superstitions and nonsense. She was, if not anything else, a sensible woman.

"What would your mother want? What will her loved ones think if you don't stop the clock, put the photos down, cover the mirrors, and—"

Timothy held up a hand to stop her. "Just do as you must." He much rather preferred that to arguing. It didn't matter to him, and it wouldn't have mattered to his mother, he was quite certain. But if it made these women rest easier, so be it.

Mrs. Jacobson brought a mug to the table and waved him over. "Please, sit down. Let us take care of everything."

Timothy again conceded. The fight was gone out of him at this point. He just hoped to make it through this day. And then the next. Until his heart stopped aching.

The women bustled about, cleaning this and that, and making the needed preparations. Or at least what they considered necessary.

After Mrs. Batson and Mrs. Jacobson were finished to their satisfaction in the great room, they joined the others in the back of the house. If only there was a way this could be done and not disrupt the grieving family—or him, in this case. But he would not dishonor his mother's memory by preventing her friends from paying their respects at the home she had loved.

He looked at the clock. Surely, they had been here longer than that. Then he remembered...Mrs. Batson stopped the clock. So, he pulled out his pocket watch. The women had invaded his home an hour ago. How much longer would it take? Then he was struck with a thought. Did one of them intend to stay overnight to sit up with Ma? As if that would make a difference in anything. But it was what was done.

Timothy splayed his hands on the rough surface of the table. So many memories here...fond times, hard times, lean times, blessed times. How would he manage to live here without Ma?

Knock, knock, knock.

The rapping on the door was softer, but insistent.

Who else would that be? How many others would disrupt his life? His privacy?

But he had to tolerate it. Maybe...just maybe it would give him a distraction. For, as it was, he tired of fighting the grief. As much as he still refused to give in to it. If he let loose his hold on his tightly controlled emotions, would he ever stop?

The knocking recommenced.

"I'm coming," he yelled. A bit louder than he'd intended. Then he looked back toward his mother's bedroom. "Are y'all expecting someone else?"

He didn't get a response. Maybe they couldn't hear him. No matter.

Gripping the latch, he swung the door wide.

And there was Jane.

Stunned and dumbfounded, he couldn't find his voice. What was she doing here? Why did she come? He was quite certain that of all the visitors today, he had the least energy for a confrontation with her.

"I'm so sorry, Timothy." She stepped to him and wrapped her arms about his shoulders, tugging him to herself.

His initial reaction was to push her away. But he didn't. Something stayed his hands. And then his arms wrapped around her. In that moment, he was overwhelmed with the full force of his pent-up emotions.

"I can't imagine what you're feeling." From the waver in her voice, he would wager that she shed tears. For him. For his loss. For his sadness.

He clung to her. And let loose the torrent. Come what may.

CHAPTER 11

The Truth

Jane tightened her shawl about her torso as Reverend Dawson closed his prayer. It was unreasonably chilly. But not as cold as the last few weeks had been. There was certainly the promise of spring in the air.

Though this was not a day to rejoice in the earth's movement toward rebirth and bloom, but to pay respects to Mrs. Johnson, the little that Jane had known her. And to stand by Timothy as he bade his mother an earthly farewell.

He had been strong during the past few days of the wake and the visiting of friends to come and honor his mother's life. But he had perhaps been too strong. Did he hold it all in? Or only find time and space to mourn in private? Since that day she came to his house, he had not given into his grief.

Was that best? What should he be like? She had been so young when her parents died. And then her aunt's death a few years back had been sad but not the same.

Those gathered around the grave began to mill about, coming to say final words to Timothy and to Reverend Dawson.

Jane stayed near but did not impose on his conversations. This was not about her. And she would not make any of it be so.

Noon loomed as the last vestiges of visitors dissipated. Reverend Dawson, as well, led his wife away and toward the main street. Perhaps for lunch. Most certainly for respite.

She turned toward Timothy to find him at the edge of his mother's grave, looking at the fresh dirt. As she neared, she heard him whispering.

"Yet I will rejoice in the Lord, I will joy in the God of my salvation."

She set a hand to his arm, gentle, tentative. "Is that Scripture?"

He nodded but did not look at her. "Habakkuk 3:18—one of my mother's favorites. When I...found her, she had been reading that chapter."

Jane rubbed his arm, hoping that spoke comfort to him.

Timothy shrugged. "At least she passed with that passage in mind."

"And we can find hope in it now."

He looked at her. "I suppose."

"It is because of God, and His work through the cross, that death does not carry the weight it once did. For we have a hope."

Timothy's gaze shifted to the horizon. As if he were deep in thought. This was not the time for such discussions. He was tired. He had just laid his mother to rest.

"Are you hungry?" Her voice seemed timid, even to her.

His mouth tightened. Then he nodded.

"Shall we grab something at the café?"

He seemed to think on that. Then shook his head.

"What sounds appetizing to you?" If not the café, where? It wasn't as if they could go back to his home, just them.

"Could we go for a walk?"

Though her stomach begged for sustenance, she would do whatever he needed. "Certainly."

She wanted to loop an arm through his but thought better of it. He may not need anything so intrusive into his thoughts. Though it could be that the stroll was for the purpose of sharing something.

Either way, she held her tongue and waited for him to speak.

"It is such a beautiful day."

"That it is." She tugged the shawl even tighter. And hoped that his need to exercise his legs wouldn't carry on for too long in this weather.

"Doesn't quite seem right, does it?"

"Nothing about these things ever seems right."

"That's true."

She concentrated on her steps, stretching her normal stride to match his longer one.

All of a sudden, he stopped.

She had continued walking and paused a couple of steps beyond him. Turning back, she watched as he glanced across the mountainous scenery and then his gaze landed on her.

"I have to be honest."

Why did his tone make her stomach lurch? "Of course."

"I have been so...thankful...these last few days. For your presence and your support."

She nodded. "I'm glad I had the opportunity."

"But I cannot deny that something isn't right."

"Oh?" Now her gut clenched.

His intense gaze bore into her then. "This is not working."

Timothy swallowed. Was he ready to push forward?

"What?" The word seemed to fall from her lips. She looked up at him, her eyes wide and shining. What did she think he meant?

He set hands on her shoulders, rubbing with his thumbs. "I can't keep pretending I..."

She bit at her lower lip. Was she eager? Distraught?

"Jane, I have always wanted a family and someone to share my life with. I can't deny that these last weeks have shown me just how much. Will you marry me?"

She looked at the ground. Was she overcome with happiness? Or preparing to turn him down? Could his heart take it if she did?

She lifted a hand to rest it on his face. "Timothy," she said, before licking her lips. "I do care for you. A great deal."

There was something unpleasant coming. He could feel it. "But...?"

"I would love to be there for you...always. And if you had mentioned me once in your proposal, I would be hard pressed."

He furrowed his brow. What did she mean? Had his words danced around her? Was that a technicality?

"As it is, I don't know that wanting a family is the right reason to get married."

His hands fell from her arms. He walked a few paces away. Were these the echoes of his conversation with Katie? For they sounded like his very words. Was this some kind of cruel cosmic joke?

"Believe me," Jane called to him on the wind, her voice sounded strained, "I do want to marry you. But I don't want to join my life with someone who only seeks a means to an end."

What could he say? What could he do? He couldn't lose her like this. Not now. Not after what they had been through.

He whirled around, rushed to close the distance between them, cupped her face, and claimed her lips. Every bit of longing he felt for her, he poured into that contact. She had to know how he felt. She needed to know.

And she responded to him, gripping his shirt, and tugging closer. She did care for him. He could feel it in the way she melted to him and the eagerness of her movements.

He released his hold on her face and let his arms enfold her. The scent of gardenias filled his senses, and the feel of her curves nearly drove him to madness. She was everything.

This was right. This was how it was supposed to be. This abandonment for the sake of someone else.

After some glorious moments of her, he broke their contact, pressing his forehead to hers.

"Tell me you don't love me back." He slid a hand back up to the side of her face to encounter moisture. Her tears must mean that she did.

The answering silence was deafening. His pulse thundered in his ears. Everything settled into this moment, into her words. If only they would come.

Unable to take it one second more, he pulled back so he could delve into her eyes.

There were many emotions on display there. So many it was difficult to determine which reigned supreme. And which would guide her response.

She laid a hand over his on her face while the other loosened its grip on his shirt and settled over his heart. "I need to tell you...I should have told you long before now. I just...didn't want it to..."

He wasn't certain what she was saying. It seemed more as if she rambled. "Jane, whatever it is, we can work through it. As long as you are by my side."

Her breath hitched as she met his gaze. "I cannot have children."

Jane watched as Timothy's features fell and his skin paled. What else could she expect?

Finally, he spoke. "What do you mean?"

She looked down, unable to face him any longer. "I...have a condition. And my doctor in San Francisco said that most women with this condition are barren."

"Then there's a chance." He didn't sound hopeful, just matter of fact. It killed her to hear his flat tone.

"The doctor said there's not enough of a chance in my case to even wish for it." She glanced back up at him.

His hand between her cheek and her hand slipped free. It was all she could do to keep from gasping at the way the simple action struck her heart. He didn't love her. He never did. She was only his way out of being alone.

Even so, she knew she would have tried to make it work if there had been any way she could satisfy what he wanted of her. Telling him was only fair. And...she wished she had done so sooner. She might have avoided entangling her heart. Her aunt's voice whispered in her mind. Perhaps this pain was her due, then.

"Jane, I..." He paused as he licked his lips. "It doesn't mean—"

"Not even you believe that," she shot out. As much as this hurt, dragging it out and pretending something different would only make it worse.

His eyes took on a tortured look. Perhaps he did care for her. At least a little. But not enough to hold her through this storm. Or place his bets on God gifting her what providence had seemed to not grant her.

He swallowed and tried again. "I feel that—"

Setting a hand to his lips, she cut him off with, "But I don't want you to." Realizing the contact, she let her hand fall. "I don't want you to feel anything. Least of all pity."

"That's not what I feel," he pressed his words out. "Just listen to me." He reached for her hand.

She pulled it back. "I've been through this, Timothy. Don't think you're the first man I've had this conversation with. I believe you want to think you can handle it. Maybe you even think that we could be together. Now. But you won't in time. You'll come to find that a life without a family—without children—is not what you want at all."

He let out a breath, as if he considered his response.

But she had had enough. There was no reason to continue to put him—or herself—through this.

"I need to go." She stepped farther away from him.

"Can't we talk about this?" He sounded so sincere. It tugged at her heart and almost gave her pause. Almost.

But she couldn't hold her rising emotion, or her tears, back any longer. So, she turned and walked away. Ran, more like it. And didn't look back.

She was out of breath when she got to the livery. A few townsfolk milled about, their curious gazes on her. Jane did her best to ignore them. What did it matter what they thought?

Gathering her strength, she spoke to the livery owner and waited for her horse. Again, she wrapped herself even more tightly in her shawl. Though it was not the wind that drove her to do so. She wanted to shrink deeper into its folds and hide. From those watching her, judging her. And from this situation. If only she could.

Soon enough, she was astride and urging the mare to return to the Sullivan homestead. Where she would undoubtedly face more questions. Unfortunately, it was the safest place she had right now. So, face them she must.

The ride to the homestead was not as long as she wished, and yet it seemed hours before she arrived. Kitty's mother was out in the vegetable garden with the two older children. Why was Lauren Matthews here? Had Wyatt had an emergency of some sort? Where were Kitty and Ellie Mae?

As Jane approached, Lauren held out a hand in her direction and spoke to Jack, who bounded over and met her outside the barn.

"I'll get her put up," he said as Jane dropped down.

At first, she wanted to argue. Maybe dealing with the horse would be a distraction. However, she soon nodded, thanking Jack for his kindness.

When she turned, Lauren was coming toward her with Susie in tow. The small girl's legs were only so long. But Lauren was patient. "How are you?" Lauren asked as she neared.

Jane felt the urge to wipe at her tears, though that might only draw attention to them. "Well."

Lauren's features scrunched as she seemed to take better note of Jane's appearance. "How is Timothy? Did the graveside service go well?"

Jane nodded. "As well as it could. He is...understandably grieving." She didn't need to tell Kitty's mother that he was more disturbed because of her revelation. All in all, he had managed these last few days well. Including the service.

"I see." Lauren watched the barn door. Did she worry after Jack?

"I...didn't expect to see you here. Is something amiss?"

"Oh, no. Wyatt needed Tom's help with a repair in the house. So, I came to see these sweet ones. After all, does a grandmother really need a reason?"

Jane smiled at that. "I suppose not." But the hollowness in her heart continued to ache.

When Jack emerged, Lauren waved him back to herself. "Why don't you take Susie inside and get her ready for her nap?"

Oh, goodness. Did this mean what it seemed? That Lauren wanted a moment to speak with Jane privately?

Jack nodded and took Susie's hand.

The little girl looked as if she would protest.

"Go with brother. If you're good, we can go see the flowers in the meadow after your nap," Lauren said. She really did have a special touch with the children.

That brightened Susie's face and she clasped Jack's hand.

"Such angels," Lauren pronounced as the two moved toward the house. "Darlings."

Jane almost clutched her chest to staunch the pain. "All children are truly."

"I've met quite a few that have a streak in them." Lauren eyed her. "I should think in your profession you have as well."

Jane offered a small smile. "I have. But I think there's always some good in there, too."

"True enough." Lauren indicated the porch. "Shall we sit for a piece?"

That was the last thing Jane wanted to do, but she didn't think refusing would accomplish anything. "Sure."

They moved up the steps and settled on a bench.

Lauren's gaze was on the horizon, but it soon shifted to Jane. "Everything all right?"

Jane wanted to nod but found she couldn't. She actually wanted —needed—someone safe to share what was in her heart. So, she looked at her hands in her lap and shrugged.

"That doesn't seem right." The woman was a mother to her core.

It made Jane's barely healed wounds from being without her mother during her formative years reopen.

Lauren set a hand to Jane's forearm. "I don't mean to pry—well, maybe I do, but I know that sometimes it is better to talk about it."

Jane nodded, keeping her eyes on her fingers. "I just...don't know where to start."

"At the beginning, of course."

Jane swallowed. Where was the beginning?

"Or perhaps you can start with Timothy. Is there something between you two?"

The force of that statement brought a wave of fresh tears.

"Oh goodness," Lauren put an arm around Jane's shoulders.

Jane leaned into her as she told the woman about her connection with Timothy and the fall out of that relationship. Lauren just listened, offering emotional support in her gentle way. And so, Jane came apart on the porch. All the while, she feared that no one, not even Lauren, would be able to fit the pieces of her life back together.

CHAPTER 12

Alone

Timothy waited until he was a good distance out of town before he pushed his horse into a gallop. Would the pounding of the horse's hooves keep him from hearing the pounding of his heart? Or his thoughts?

What was he going to do...with his heart, with his life, with his future? If Jane was not his future, did he have one? Did anyone care about him at this point? Truly?

There would be no one there when he got to his homestead, and no one to wake up for tomorrow. Things had gone from bad...to worse.

Maybe he needed to pack up and start anew somewhere else. Yes, that might just be it. For there was nothing holding him here. Not anymore.

He slowed the horse as he approached the house that had been his parents' home for so many years. Yes, it was theirs. Not truly his. Perhaps it could have been, but he doubted it.

Should he gather a few things and head off tonight? He dropped out of the saddle. Perhaps so. He'd just have to hitch the wagon and then he'd be gone.

Maybe an hour then.

Something nagged at him, telling him that this was impulsive, a reaction to the terrible thing that had just happened—both his mother's passing and what Jane revealed. Now was not the time to make life decisions. One should really sleep on news such as he had been hit with.

How much did he care for Jane?

There was no question—he loved her. But was she right? That he would give up on her in a matter of days or weeks? He did not know. The desire to have a family had always been so strong within him. Even when he'd lost hope of finding love. And now, even that was crushed. Again.

Yes, it would be best if he put this town and these problems behind himself.

He tied the reins to a post and rushed for the front door.

Just then, a movement beside the barn caught his eye. And he paused.

What was that?

He squinted to try to home in on whatever it might be.

Nothing.

But as he pushed the front door open, he could've sworn he heard rustling in the grass.

There was something there. Was it some*one*? He'd do best to surprise whomever it might be.

Slipping into the house, he grabbed his father's rifle and moved toward the back of the house. The kitchen door was the best option to sneak around the outside and with any luck, come upon the intruder.

He opened the kitchen door slowly, cringing as the hinges squeaked. It wasn't loud, but it was there. Why had he delayed oiling them when his mother asked him to? Pushing that thought to the side, he continued out to the back of the house.

As he crept around to the side, he looked around the corner, searching near the barn and along the outer wall of the homestead. Nothing.

He started to think it may have all been in his mind. Perhaps he was too worn to make any worthwhile decisions.

Best he stayed on alert and finish his walk around the perimeter before he gave up.

Walking along the outer wall, he kept his rifle at the ready. No need to take any chances.

He neared the front porch and all but decided he had conjured the noise.

But a twig snapped around the corner, near the front door. Had the riffraff decided to sneak into the house and surprise *him*?

He leveled the rifle and led with the gun as he neared the front corner. Just a little farther.

And as he peered around, he spotted the interloper—a boy of maybe ten or eleven. The youngster's steps were uneven and cautious as he tried to peek in through the front window.

"What are you doing here?" he bellowed as he lowered his gun only slightly. No way to know if the boy had accomplices.

The lad froze. But there was something familiar about him.

Holding out his hands, the boy turned.

It was Lemuel.

Jane picked up the last of the dinner dishes and moved them to the sink. Then she let her gaze wander to the great room. Such a happy scene.

Lauren knelt beside Susie and Ellie Mae, engaged in a rather animated retelling of *Cinderella*. Kitty's father was settled with Jack to one side, fairly amused. Wyatt and Kitty had moved their large chairs closer so they could hold hands while they listened.

It was the perfect picture of what a family should be. A picture of what Jane would never have. What God had determined she would never have.

And why not? Hadn't she suffered enough? Why didn't she get a happily ever after?

Enough of that! she chided herself. This was a scene to be treasured, revered even. Not a place to find reason to scorn her own predicament. Didn't she care for her friend enough to be happy for her situation? She did.

But Jane couldn't fight the whole of her sadness. And so, she let her grief be what it was.

The family in front of her was a close-knit group. They had come together more than once to make life easier for each other. And it made them strong.

Jane reminded herself that she had never known that. How could she truly know what she missed?

But she did.

Maybe it was time for her to return to San Francisco. After all, she had not intended to stay so long in Cripple Creek. Her... Actually, no one waited for her or missed her in San Francisco.

Still, there was little reason to stay.

She turned away from the happy scene and washed the dishes. It was something helpful she could do. Focusing on her task, she didn't know the gathering had ended until someone came up behind her.

"You are such a blessing, Jane dear."

Jane turned. It was Lauren, beaming at her.

"You are one to say so. But I suppose you know how that is." Jane offered her a tired smile. "Thank you for listening."

Lauren put a hand on Jane's shoulder. "Anytime."

Jane wiped at the sink edge with a towel.

Lauren moved back to let Jane hang the towel to dry. "Do you realize what a godsend you have been—to this town and to this family?"

Jane shrugged. "I do what I can."

"You do more than that. I don't know what would have happened with Katie if you hadn't made Wyatt see reason. And what of those children? No teacher to guide them."

"It's only temporary. I was happy to step in."

"Exactly. That's what I mean. You are so selfless. It would be all right, you know, to need others every now and again."

"I appreciate that." Part of her wanted to speak further. About how no one had ever seemed even the least bit interested in what she needed. But she decided she had leaned on Lauren enough this day.

"And we appreciate you." Lauren's smile was genuine.

Tom came up behind his wife. "We'd best get home. I'm sure them bed bugs will be missing us."

"Oh, fie," Lauren said, swatting at Tom. "You shouldn't joke about that."

He set hands to his wife's shoulders and pressed a kiss to her hair.

Just one more happy couple. But even as Jane's heart ached, she was happy for them.

"Jane," Kitty called from the great room. "I totally forgot to tell you..."

Jane came around Lauren and Tom to look at her friend. "What is it?"

"You got a letter today." Kitty rummaged through the papers on a side table. "Ah, here it is."

Jane stepped forward to intercept it.

"Someone from San Francisco it seems." Kitty gave her a half smile. "Hope they aren't calling you back so soon."

Jane forced a laugh. "I'm sure that's not the case."

Kitty waved her mother in for a hug as Lauren and Tom moved toward the door.

"Good evening to you both," Jane called as she moved to the dining table, eager to see who the letter was from. The return address was written hastily. Indeed, it was from San Francisco, but that was about all she could make out.

She tore at the seal and slid the folded papers out. Then glanced first at the salutation and signature—Frank.

What could he want? And after weeks of not hearing anything.

She folded the slips and slid them back into the envelope. Did she care to read it? Or should she just dispose of it? How was she to know?

"From a friend?" Kitty asked from just inside the front door. She had closed it after ushering her parents out.

Jane nodded. "Nothing important."

Kitty grinned. "Good. I'd hate for someone to be rushing you back."

It was odd, sometimes Kitty seemed or acted so normal. Then there were days that were worse. Much worse.

"Unless you need something, I think I'll retire for the night."

Kitty watched her. "Everything all right?"

What to do? Be honest? That might just weigh Kitty unnecessarily. She'd had a few good days in a row. It didn't seem worth the risk. So, Jane nodded. "Just tired."

Kitty seemed placated enough, so Jane made her way to her borrowed bedroom with the letter in hand. A letter she wasn't certain she should keep.

Timothy sucked in a breath. The cold metal of the rifle chilled his skin. What if he had used the gun? On this boy? What would have happened?

"What are you doing here?" He pushed out, fear still creeping over him and making his tone harsher than intended.

Lemuel looked at him...and the rifle, eyes widened. Did he imagine how this could have gone?

"Is something wrong?" Timothy searched Lemuel's face and body. Had his pa beat him? Was he badly injured? What might Timothy do? Then he noticed the lad had been favoring his right leg. "What happened to your leg?"

Lemuel's face reddened.

Anger rose in Timothy. How could he send this boy back to his father now? What was he to do? Keep the youngster here?

Then what? It wasn't an easy thing to remove a child from their parent.

Maybe he could make his future more of a sacrifice...take Lemuel with him. That would keep the boy safe.

The wind whipped about them...not doing anything to help with his chill.

"Tell me." Timothy licked his lips, which had become dry. "Why are you here?"

Lemuel swallowed, his throat bobbed. Why was he so reluctant? He came here for some reason. Would he now refuse to speak?

"I...didn't know where to go. Or who to trust." The words were pressed out with a shaky voice.

Timothy set the rifle against the side of the house. And set a hand on Lemuel's shoulder.

The boy shrunk back.

Timothy hated that. He had intended the gesture to be reassuring. "You can trust me."

Lemuel looked down, as if gauging the truth of Timothy's statement. Or trying to muster the courage to speak.

Timothy wanted to say something, but he felt it best to give Lemuel the space to talk as he could.

"My...my Pa is in a bad way."

That was certainly an understatement. Timothy tried to keep his voice even and calm. "What do you mean?"

"He's been drinking." Lemuel peered up at Timothy as if to watch his reaction. As if this bit of information was news.

Timothy kept his features stagnant. No reaction was better than forcing one.

"But I ain't never seen him quite like this."

Timothy's heart ached for the youngster. Had his father visited uncharacteristic wrath upon him? Still, Timothy held his tongue and waited.

"He fell. Hard. I don't know..." Lemuel's eyes misted.

Timothy squeezed his shoulder. "Take me to him."

The boy nodded, sniffling and wiping at his face with his sleeve.

Timothy admired how brave the boy was. It showed a strength beyond what Timothy had expected.

Lemuel moved to pass Timothy. Would he lead on foot?

It would be best to take the horse. But then again, not knowing what he might find, Timothy thought better about it. The wagon would give him more options. "Let me hitch up the wagon real quick."

The boy nodded and followed as Timothy grabbed his horse's reins and led the animal toward the barn.

With Lemuel's help, the wagon was hitched in record time, despite the fact that Timothy would rather it not be. The sense of urgency within him was quelled by apprehension of what he might find.

Lemuel climbed up to the driver's box and Timothy did the same. The ride to the property was quiet...the tension drawing thin. Did the boy fear what would be discovered as well?

As they came to a stop, Timothy was surprised at the disarray that met him. The house had been poorly maintained. Though he wasn't sure that he'd expected anything different.

He pressed that to the side and dropped down. Coming around the cart to assist Lemuel, he found the boy halfway to the ground already.

Taking a minute to think, Timothy wondered if Lemuel should remain outside. The uncertainty of the situation bade him to try and make the lad wait. But how to propose such?

"I need you to stay with the horse. She gets pretty anxious in new places."

Lemuel's eyes narrowed slightly. Did he know it was a ploy? Would he care? After a moment, the lines in his face smoothed. And Timothy breathed a sigh of relief.

"I'll keep her company." The words came stiffly.

Timothy nodded and cautiously walked up the rickety steps of the porch to the front door. If he had thought the schoolhouse had been in bad shape...

Pushing that thought from his mind, he slipped through the door that hung by one hinge. The house was just as cold on the inside, if not colder. How did Lemuel survive the winter like this? Timothy glanced at the hearth, it looked like it hadn't had a fire in weeks. Probably longer.

"Mr..." What was Lemuel's surname? Timothy realized he didn't know it. "Hello?"

No answer.

He pushed through the strewn about furniture in the great room and stepped into the kitchen. Nothing there.

"Hello?" he called again, louder.

No answer again.

He maneuvered through the area. His skin crawled at the thought of Lemuel living here, struggling to survive. The kitchen had little food and nothing of any substance. How could a man so completely give up? What had led to this?

Timothy drew in a deep breath and stepped toward the one doorway. As he came to the threshold, he spotted Lemuel's pa. Legs poked out from the opposite side of the bed.

"Sir?" Timothy tried again, not truly expecting an answer.

Nothing.

Lord...

Timothy didn't quite know what to pray, but he sent up the word, hoping that God would understand his heart. Lemuel didn't deserve this kind of life. No child did.

As he came around the bed, he found Lemuel's father, his body at an odd angle and his head bleeding. A bed table lay on its side near his head. Had he crashed into it? Headfirst?

Timothy wanted to return to Lemuel and take him from this horrid situation, but he knew better. So, he moved around the obstacles and crouched by the man. Now Timothy recognized him—Mr.

Langley. He and his wife had been regular churchgoers before the typhoid when...

The pieces fell into place. Mrs. Langley had been one of the townspeople lost to the dreadful epidemic. Is that what happened here? The man sinking into a dark place in his grief?

Timothy leaned over him, searching for any sign that the man still breathed. There didn't seem to be any movement of any kind. Setting a hand to the man's roughened wrist, he hoped against hope to find some evidence there.

Nothing discernable.

Timothy took off his hat and said a prayer over the man.

CHAPTER 13

Hope

J ane stood as the last note of the final hymn faded. It had been a good service. Reverend Dawson's words of encouragement and challenge had been sorely needed. They were a balm for Jane's soul. He had talked about being faithful where God's plans have placed each person—reinforcing that there is a purpose in it. The reverend visited the book of Nehemiah in his message. It was a perspective she hadn't heard before, but it was good.

Nehemiah had been obedient with what God set in front of him. In every circumstance. And then God enlarged His calling on Nehemiah. Could God use her where she was? It was true that the precious children at the school needed her. Maybe for more than just a temporary situation. Perhaps *that* was God's way of granting her heart's desire.

Between Lauren's words the previous evening and the conviction being visited upon her heart now, it seemed she should stay. Would the mayor and the town council consider offering her the position permanently?

Would that be wise—what with the prospect of coming across Timothy from time to time? Perhaps watching him meet someone else...then court and marry this person, giving her all the things that

Jane couldn't have. It wouldn't be fair to begrudge him that. Every man wanted a family. Why would she wish Timothy to have anything less than everything he wanted? She loved him and wanted every happiness for him.

Still, that didn't change her wish to not watch it happen. Yet was that reason enough to give up where God had called her?

"You are deep in thought." The voice belonged to Kat.

Jane shifted to meet her friend's gaze. "As a fact, I am."

"Anything you want to share?" Kitty's smile was genuine. How could Jane bring her down with the thoughts swirling within? No, she wished to prolong Kitty's happy mood.

"It's nothing. Just daydreams."

"Oh?" Kitty's smile faltered, and her voice softened. "Are you thinking about Timothy?"

How could Jane lie when her friend clearly knew her so well? "Perhaps."

Kitty set a hand on Jane's arm. "Don't let it weigh on you."

Jane had shared only bits and pieces with Kat. Again, it was an effort to keep Kitty's mood up. But it felt dishonest. And untrusting.

"God has a plan here. And He will work everything out." Kitty's smile widened again. "That's what faith is all about."

Why did faith have to be the harder road—trusting when things seemed hopeless?

Kitty picked up Ellie Mae and snagged Jane's arm as she moved into the center aisle. Jack took Susie by the hand from the pew on the opposite side, where they had sat with Lauren and Tom. They had all pitched in to help Kitty manage the children today. Wyatt had apparently been called away in the night for a medical emergency of some sort. Was he still at the clinic? Or back home resting?

But that was not Jane's concern. Certainly not with her own challenges staring her in the face. Had she even decided what to do? If she did wish to fill the teaching position, she'd best speak with the mayor sooner rather than later. She halted, causing Kitty to stop as well.

Kitty looked back at her. "What is it?"

"I...need to speak with Mayor Jacobson for a moment."

"Sure. Want me to come with you?"

"No, thank you, but that's not necessary."

Why Kitty wanted to come or what she thought Jane intended to say was a mystery. Maybe it was only Kitty's protective nature.

Kitty nodded, but there was a flash of apprehension in her eyes. Jane decided not to think too much on it or put too much stock in it. She needed to do what was right and good for herself according to what God had set in front of her.

Jane parted company with Kat, assuring she would find Kitty again momentarily. Then she glanced about for the mayor. It took a bit of time to locate him. He had just finished speaking with Reverend Dawson at the exit and was even then moving off.

Picking up pace, Jane joined the line of townsfolk waiting to shake hands with the reverend before departing. If only there were another way—a shorter way—to exit. But there wasn't.

So, she stood as patiently as she could and prayed that Mayor Jacobson would still be milling about outside when she finished.

The seconds ticked by and when Jane was next in line, she felt antsy enough to pull her hair out.

Mrs. Batson was in front of her—the last obstacle to the field beyond the church.

"My, Reverend, what a good word you brought us today. I wonder, however, about that passage. I can't say as I remember some of those verses as well as I used to. Do you think that...?"

The woman droned on. It seemed as if her string of words might never form a question. Certainly not one that anybody would be able to follow.

Jane gritted her teeth as the time stretched into minutes. Did the woman not realize others waited?

It was all she could do to keep from excusing herself and passing around the woman.

But as Jane garnered enough courage to do just that, Mrs. Batson said, "Thank you, Reverend. I think I'll move along. Try to catch dear Mrs. Jacobson."

Oh, dear. The woman would then monopolize the mayor's wife and possibly the mayor. Jane couldn't allow it. She might very well lose her nerve and her final vestiges of patience.

Sticking her hand forth, Jane murmured her thanks to the preacher and moved on.

Mrs. Batson was crossing in front of the church. To where? Had she spotted the Jacobsons?

As Jane scanned the area, she indeed saw that the older woman made straight for the mayor and his wife. How was Jane to get around her without being obtuse?

Jane picked up her step, hoping that the woman would be delayed or detained by another friend along the way. Even as Jane stretched her stride, it seemed unlikely she would make it to Mayor Jacobson first. Mrs. Batson was within calling distance and opened her mouth to do just that.

"Yoo-hoo!" The voice was not Mrs. Batson's, but another, slightly younger woman trying to get Mrs. Batson's attention.

Curiosity tugged at Jane, but she forced her attention to remain on her target. And shot past Mrs. Batson as she attempted to find the source of the entreaty.

Jane closed the distance to the mayor and sucked in a breath.

"Mr. Jacobson," she pressed out, trying to control her breathing and not pant.

The mayor turned and his gaze lit up. "Miss Millington."

His wife gave his arm a squeeze and spoke quietly to him before moving off. Indeed, she went to where Mrs. Batson and the other woman stood chatting.

Jane paused and somehow kept from doubling over, as winded as she was.

"Miss Millington, I was hoping to find you today."

"You were?" Jane could do nothing about her surprise being on display, she was too focused on not heaving.

"Yes, I have great news." He smiled.

Great news? What could he mean?

"The new teacher will be here by Friday. And she'll be ready to take over the schoolhouse that following Monday."

Jane's breath caught. The new teacher was already en route? Her heart fell as the way before her had been effectively cut off. "Oh."

"Isn't that wonderful news?" His features creased as if he were confused at her reaction.

"Oh, yes. That's...wonderful." She couldn't think of a different word in that moment.

"We have much appreciated you stepping in during the interim. So very grateful. The new teacher was an easier find than I had thought."

She nodded. Just perfect. But she tried to disguise her disappointment as much as possible.

"What did you need to speak to me about?"

Oh, yes, she had sought him out. What could she say? Certainly not what was in her heart and on her mind. Why would God offer her a place to belong only to then snatch it away?

"I...um, was wondering about the repairs." She wanted to take her words back as soon as they were out. How insensitive she must seem...worried about repairs when Timothy had just yesterday laid his mother to rest. "That is...I understand if Mr. Johnson will no longer be able to complete them. But there are several things that need to be addressed still."

"Of course." The mayor's brow furrowed. "I had been thinking on the same thing as well. Especially with the new teacher coming. It would be nice to have a fully repaired schoolhouse to present to her. Let me make some more inquiries today. I might be able to find someone who can step in."

She nodded, feeling bad at how she must appear with her concerns. "Thank you, Mayor. I hope you have a pleasant day." Then she tipped her head and moved off.

True, her behavior was odd, but she couldn't let him see...

couldn't let him know that she was crumbling to pieces within. Where would she belong now?

Timothy closed the door to one of the clinic's recovery rooms with as much ease as possible. How Lemuel fought sleep for so long was beyond him. The boy had been tired and weary even before this whole drama with his pa. Lemuel was either very concerned after his pa, or very worried what his pa might do to punish him for any misstep. Perhaps both. That couldn't be easy. And Timothy's heart went out to him.

They had sat untold hours while Wyatt and Mr. Taylor worked on Mr. Langley. Timothy wasn't certain what had happened with Lemuel's father through the night, but if he did live, Timothy was sure the man barely clung to life.

Making his way to the main clinic area, Timothy hoped he might find Wyatt. That thought surprised him. He had spent the better part of the last year avoiding Wyatt, now he sought the man out. Perhaps his care for Lemuel was greater than his consideration for old wounds.

He stepped off the last stair to an empty room. The strong smell of medicinals filled the space. How many things did Wyatt have to try? Timothy didn't remember some of these smells being present before.

Moving about the room to keep himself awake, Timothy found himself praying for the man again. And for Lemuel. What was this? He had been certain that prayer was a thing of the past. Yet here he was. And had been, he realized. His prayers for this broken family had been prevalent over the night's activities.

The door creaked and Wyatt appeared.

Timothy swallowed. As much as he wished to know the state of things, he still did not want to face Wyatt.

"Oh, you're still awake." Wyatt's words were slow and measured.

More likely due to his own fatigue. The man had lines about his eyes that were not from age.

"Yes." Timothy shifted his weight from one foot to another. "I finally got Lemuel to lie down."

"He seems pretty worried about his pa."

Timothy nodded but didn't speak to that. "How is Mr. Langley?"

Wyatt shook his head as he leaned against the exam table, crossing his arms. "It's bad. About the worst case of overdrinking I've seen. And the head wound doesn't make matters any better."

Timothy swallowed. He didn't care for this casual air between him and Wyatt. But that wasn't important right now. "What are his chances?"

"It's too soon to say." Wyatt leveled his gaze on Timothy. "I stitched up his head. That's taken care of...though I'm not sure the extent of the internal damage. Mr. Taylor helped get some water into him...as much as possible. He's still in there, waiting for Mr. Langley to regain consciousness. If he will."

Timothy didn't know what to want in this situation. He didn't want Mr. Langley to die, but he wasn't sure that he could let Lemuel go back into that life.

"I think he may yet pull through though." Wyatt yawned then.

"What happens then?"

"I'll give him a stiff lecture about the dangers of drinking so much, but then he'll go home. There's not much else I can do." Wyatt shrugged.

"What of the boy?"

"What do you mean?" Wyatt's tone sounded as if he were confused. "He'll return home with his pa."

Timothy glanced at the floor. How much did he trust Wyatt? Certainly not as much as he had in years past. But he needed to speak further on Lemuel's behalf. "I'm not so sure that's a good idea."

Wyatt's brow furrowed and his features betrayed an edge of worry. "Why not?"

"The place is ill kept. And there is reason to believe the man isn't taking care of the boy. In fact..." Timothy paused, earning a glower from Wyatt.

"That's quite the accusation." Wyatt's words had softened. "I don't want the boy to suffer, but there's only so much we can do if Mr. Langley pulls through. He's the child's father."

Timothy closed his eyes and took a deep breath before opening them and continuing. "I think Mr. Langley may be taking his anger out on the boy."

Wyatt didn't answer for several seconds. A mixture of emotions passed over his features. Most likely from his own memories of being injured at his father's hands. "I understand your concern. And as much as I want to protect the boy, we would need some evidence to prove that before I could take action."

Why would Wyatt...of all people...not be more helpful? He knew very well and good what that kind of life was for a defenseless child.

"I have seen bruises on the boy. And even now he has a limp. The child is terrified of his pa. Can't you see it all add up?"

Wyatt frowned. "That may be. But it's easy to misread these things. Let's wait until we look into this more. Maybe I'll have a chat with Lemuel when he wakes."

"A chat?" Timothy scoffed. "You think he'll tell you what's going on?"

"I think he might."

Timothy pressed his fist into his hand. This was not going well.

Wyatt took advantage of the pause. "Look, I know what that's like to hide. To be ashamed. And maybe I can get him to say things he wouldn't say to a reverend."

"I'm not a reverend." Timothy's words were spat out and harsher than he'd wanted them to be.

"I know that. But as far as most of this town is concerned—including the children that watched you lay their loved ones to rest after the plague—you always will be."

Timothy had not considered that. Perhaps Wyatt had a point.

Either way, more tension between them would not help Lemuel. He pushed out a breath.

"Listen, I didn't mean to antagonize you." Wyatt's tone had evened out again. "I just...it's nice to see my friend walking in his calling again...caring about people."

Timothy wanted to balk. Was Wyatt saying he had stopped caring about others? He pulled words together to shoot back at the doctor but stopped himself. Was it true? Had he been so caught up in his own pain that he shoved all else to the side—God and others included?

"Like I said, I don't mean to antagonize you," Wyatt said as he unfolded his arms. "I just hope that someday you can take a step back. Maybe forgive Katie and me. And yourself."

Forgive himself? Timothy's eyes widened. What had he to take blame for? To feel bad about? But he knew. He couldn't hide from his own self-condemnation. He'd not taken Katie's offer to marry. He'd tried to infringe on a marriage. It was not easy to face that.

Wyatt spoke again, his words even more gentle. "But more than anything, I don't want to see you make the same mistakes."

Timothy glared at Wyatt, wishing he could wipe that knowing look off the man's face. What did Wyatt know? What did he care?

Yet his words and his boldness made it seem as if he did.

"I need some air." Timothy spun and stepped to the door. But as he put a hand to the latch, Wyatt spoke again.

"Don't let your inability to let go of the past ruin your hope for the future."

Timothy wanted to just walk away, but he found he couldn't. "You don't know what you think you know," he said gruffly. Then he opened the door and flung it closed behind himself.

Jane dropped down from her mare, curious about the horse and cart at the front of the school. It didn't look familiar. But who would have come other than Timothy?

A shiver ran down her back, she wasn't altogether certain she was ready to face him. Not yet. Maybe not ever. Should she wait out here for him to finish? She couldn't imagine he would be so bold as to face her down either.

But as she stood near the open door, she caught two distinct voices. They, too, sounded familiar. If only there were enough back and forth between them for her catch. But the sawing and hammering made their identities much more difficult to discern.

She sighed. There was nothing more for her to do than just go on in. Swallowing, then squaring her shoulders, she marched up the now repaired steps and into the schoolhouse.

Tom Matthews and his son were within, leaning over the place in the floor that had once had a hole. It was all but covered with fresh boards.

"Miss Millington," Kitty's brother called, having looked up from his work and spotted her.

She shook herself free of her stupor. "Mr. Matthews, I'm quite certain you can call me Jane."

"And you had best call me David." He smiled—the kind of smile that likely had his wife's heart fluttering.

She nodded and shifted her focus to Kitty's father. "What's going on here?"

"I should think that was quite obvious." Tom's features lightened. "We're fixing this floor."

"But why?" She maneuvered around the desks to stand next to the two men.

"Well, it needs to be done." Tom again took the lead.

"That is true. But I thought..." Jane couldn't find her words.

"No need to worry with us. We'll be finished before lessons start."

"That's not what I'm concerned about."

"Oh?" David looked to his father and back to her. "The mayor was pretty adamant that you needed some repairs done. He wasn't wrong—this schoolhouse is a sight."

"Yes." Jane let out a breath. It wasn't something to really concern herself over—who did the repairs. She might should even be grateful that she wouldn't be crossing paths with Timothy today. Perhaps never again.

"Now, get to your own preparations," Kitty's father said. "Don't you mind us one bit. Besides, we're about done with this floor."

"All right." She took tentative steps to her desk, settling into the chair. Only then did she realize she hadn't taken her coat off. So, she got up and walked to the back of the room to hang her coat on a peg there. In the next week or so it would be warm enough to come without any outerwear. Then again...she wouldn't be here next week.

Jane ran a hand down her coat, feeling the full measure of her limited time here. Where would she go then? She shook her head and stepped back to her desk. After sitting, she looked through the stack of books, trying to remind herself what she was teaching today.

"It's going to be a bit loud for a few minutes," David called over his shoulder.

She waved them off. What else could she do? Tell them to hammer gently? Smiling to herself, she bent over the writing volume. What would she have the children practice today?

It wasn't long before she felt as if she were being watched.

Jerking her focus up, she saw that Timothy stood just inside the schoolhouse. How had she missed him opening and closing the door? Oh yes, the confounded hammering.

She rose, opening her mouth to speak, but no words would come.

His features were drawn and strained. He did not look happy.

What was she to say? What could she do? Dare she hope he was here to say something to her? To take back what had happened before? Profess a love for her?

"What are they doing?" He indicated the Matthews father and son team.

She glanced at them to see that they had slowed and watched Timothy as well. "The mayor asked them to assist with the repairs. He...thought you might need to take a few days."

Timothy rubbed the bridge of his nose. "Is everyone in this town going to make decisions for me now?"

An anchor weighed in the bottom of Jane's stomach. It really was that bad. Timothy was here, not to say he loved her, but to work. Only, Tom and David had effectively usurped him.

Movement beside Timothy drew her attention. Lemuel shuffled around him to get to his desk.

Timothy nodded at him, setting a hand to his shoulder, and speaking to him briefly. Then he stood to his full height. "I see you've got this all under control."

Who was he speaking to? Her or Tom and David?

"I suppose I'll take my leave now as I am not needed."

He spun and marched to the door, but as he stepped outside, he took care to close it gently.

Jane grasped for something to say. What he had said wasn't true...and it hurt her that he believed he wasn't needed. And that he thought she had thwarted his work.

Without a further thought she rushed after him.

Timothy pushed on. Why had he come? What had he expected? He just hadn't planned for her to be so alluring. For her presence to strike him so fully out of tongue.

He wasn't certain why he had lashed out. It just seemed the best way to distance her. Was that really what he wanted?

"Timothy!"

It was Jane's voice. Was she coming after him? *Heaven, help me.*

These little snippets of prayer were becoming more frequent.

But dare he turn and intercept her? Or make her keep pursuing him?

He considered it as he pressed onward.

This is nonsense.

Pausing, he shifted to face the schoolhouse. And her approaching figure.

"Timothy," she said between puffs of air. Had she exerted herself too much?

He just waited on her to come to him. Not moving, not speaking. Like a coward.

"You have to know it wasn't like that," she managed.

"Like what?" He could kick himself. Must he now play games with her?

"It's not as if you aren't needed. The mayor just...wanted everything ready for the new teacher."

He widened his eyes. "They found another teacher?"

She nodded, but her movements were reluctant. "She'll be here Friday."

What was he to do with this information? It struck him, right in the chest. "What will you do?"

That was rather forward, but he couldn't keep himself from asking.

"I don't know," she said, looking down at her hands. "I suppose I'll go back to San Francisco."

That drove a barb into his heart. "To San Francisco?"

She shrugged. It seemed as if she didn't want to have this conversation either. But felt compelled the same as he.

"But...you said there is nothing there for you." The words were out before he could stop them. He wasn't guarding his heart very well. Though it was difficult with the breeze teasing him with the scent of gardenias from her hair. Did she wash with flower blooms?

She peered up at him. "There's nothing here for me."

As if a knife twisted in his gut, he bit at the inside of his lip. "You have Katie...er, Katherine."

Jane looked away, toward the cluster of buildings that made up the main street.

"You don't have to go because of me."

She glared at him then. "You think that's it? That I'm leaving because of you?" Her laugh was broken and seemed forced.

"Aren't you?" He pressed into the tense moment.

Her eyes glistened as she stared at him. Would she deny it again?

"Perhaps." She rubbed her arms. In her haste, she had left her coat behind.

Though he didn't feel right about offering his, it seemed wrong not to. So, he tugged at his sleeve, freeing his right arm.

"Don't." Jane looked as if she were on the verge of tears.

He halted, not sure of how to proceed, but put his arm back in the vacated sleeve. It seemed odd for them to have this private moment in the open here. "Let me walk you back to the schoolhouse. The children will be here soon."

She nodded and took up step beside him.

He relished the closeness of their bodies, but he knew it would only haunt him for the rest of the day. Yet, he had to ask more.

"I wondered if you have noticed anything...off...about Lemuel."

She cleared her throat. "Off? How do you mean?"

"I don't know. Strange behaviors, injuries, anything?" He didn't want to worry her or lead her to think more on something that was nothing. But if she had noticed, they might both be able to convince the mayor that Lemuel was not safe with his father.

"He is often tired. Doesn't really interact well with others. Especially me. He seems standoffish almost. But he has a group of friends. And they sometimes get into trouble."

Timothy was quiet for a moment. That wasn't exactly what he had hoped for.

They neared the school building, and he heard the voices of children headed their way.

"Thank you. Just...let me know if you think of anything else."

She nodded. "What's happened?"

Should he trust her with this? It may create another connection between them. That was the last thing he needed.

"His father is in the clinic. And Wyatt isn't certain how things will go with him. But he's doing better and things look hopeful."

Her brow furrowed. "That's good news. Isn't it?"

She was perceptive. More than he gave her credit for.

He nodded.

The childlike voices drew near. And the sounds of hammering within had subsided. The two men would likely emerge soon.

"Have a good day," he murmured before turning toward town.

"Timothy, wait..."

He paused, shifting to look at her once more.

She chewed on her bottom lip. But didn't say anything. Though the war within her was quite obvious.

His hands itched to touch her, for even just a moment. Still, he knew that would only make things worse. "I'm sorry," he blurted.

Her eyes widened and moisture gathered in them.

"I wish things could have been different." With that, he moved off. And though everything in him screamed to do so, he did not look back.

Jane directed the horse as they neared the Sullivan homestead. It was difficult to cut through the emotions within her to see straight. No wonder the animal meandered a bit. She must give it better direction.

But the last hour had been taxing. And overwhelming.

She had waited for Timothy at the end of the day, hoping that they could speak when he picked up Lemuel. Or at least they would exchange a look, a touch, something. But there was no such interaction.

He waited outside the schoolhouse. She spied him through the window. As did Lemuel. So, when she released the class for the day, Lemuel rushed from the room. Then he and Timothy disappeared in the resulting mayhem.

Did Timothy not feel for her more than that? Such that he could so easily disregard her and her feelings?

This was nonsense. He had made himself perfectly clear. Why would she still hold onto hope? In vain.

Perhaps she should entertain Frank's words, whatever they were. She had set aside his letter, for good she thought. Though it remained in her journal, tucked between the pages. Maybe she hadn't completely dismissed him, then. That may be for the best.

Did she have the courage to read the letter? Would Frank repeat his earlier sentiments? That seemed unlikely. If so, why would he bother writing? He must have changed his mind.

The homestead came into view. Only...an additional cart sat near the porch. What additional surprise awaited her? She didn't like the unexpected. Certainly not twice in one day. Finding Tom and David busy with repairs had been a pleasant surprise but jarring all the same. As well, it reminded her that the schoolhouse would not be hers much longer.

Urging the horse the rest of the way, she prayed for God to ease her anxious heart. It wouldn't do for her to create more problems in the precarious situation. Kitty was doing better, that was true. But Jane feared she might revert to her earlier state at any moment.

The sun, now lower in the sky, seemed to welcome her to the homestead. It also illuminated the children playing in the yard. Among them, were Kitty's niece and nephew. Had David come here as well? The cart didn't look the same.

She neared and dropped from the animal's back.

Jack was ready and eager to take the reins. "I'll get her to the barn."

"Thank you." She sputtered as she eyed Jessie and Peter playing with their younger cousins. How had they arrived before her? Perhaps their mother or father brought them straight here after school.

Jane wanted to ask Jack about their presence, but he was off before she could find the words. So, she smiled at the children and nodded in their direction as she climbed the few steps to the porch.

The front door burst open as she reached for the latch.

And she nearly collided with Mary Matthews.

"Oh dear," Mary said as she backed up a step. No easy task with the house rugs piled atop her arms. "Pardon me!"

Jane smiled, but an uneasiness settled in her stomach. What was going on here?

Mary sidestepped with her load, carrying them to the edge of the porch.

Jane pressed into the house.

The smell of chicken and dumplings filled the great room and kitchen. Had someone made dinner? Mary perhaps?

Lauren was busy sweeping, but she looked up. "Hello, Jane. How was school today?"

Jane nodded. "It was fine." How would her lie come across? For everything in her fairly mourned one more day gone. The last of her days with the children in this town.

Kitty's mother continued her work, looking down at the floor. "That's nice."

Then she hadn't caught the emotion in Jane's voice. Jane didn't know if her heart was relieved or sad that her grief had escaped notice.

Kitty came from the bedroom then. "Ma, I can't find the..." Her sentence cut off as she spotted Jane. "Isn't it wonderful, Jane? Ma and Mary came over to clean the house. I don't deserve either of them."

Clean the house? Had Jane not done an adequate job? True, her attention—and time—had been divided between school preparations, school hours, and being there for Timothy. But she had done the best she could. Was it not enough?

When she looked up again, she saw that Kitty was watching her.

"Is something the matter?" Kitty's words seemed worried.

"It's nothing. I just..." As Jane searched for the right words, a loud *whomp* split the air.

"Oh, don't worry." Kitty waved a hand. "That's just Mary beating the tar out of those rugs. And my did they ever need it."

"I didn't see Wyatt." Jane wondered out loud. "Is he resting?" She hoped not. For that sound likely woke him.

Kitty moved to the dining table, wiping the surface with a cloth she had been holding. "He came back earlier today, slept for a few hours, and went back to the clinic. He has a patient in a bad way."

"Oh." Should she tell Kitty that it was Mr. Langley? If Wyatt didn't, she best not. "Is...there anything I can help with?" Though her body ached to lie down, she felt responsible.

"Ma, there's a spot here." Kitty rubbed vigorously at the table.

Jane sighed. That was one of the places Susie had spilled syrup. Had she missed getting it all up?

"Let me see," Lauren set the broom against a wall and stepped closer to the table. "I see. We might need to get that cloth wet and set it over that for a minute or two."

Jane watched as Kitty and Lauren continued to chat and then moved into a rhythm with the cleaning that did not include her. She was, as it seemed, all but forgotten.

"I'm just going to lie down for a minute," Jane said a bit louder.

Kitty laughed at something her mother had said.

Indeed, it was as if Jane weren't there at all. Pushing her feet forward, one right after the other, she soon slipped into the solace of her borrowed bedroom. Not her room...just a loaned bed to accommodate her. For how much longer? Would it be right to linger after she was no longer needed at the school? She may have overstayed her welcome as it was.

She closed the door, trying to seal out the pleasant family interaction. The kind she had never had and never would.

Stopping herself, she groaned. This was not the time to be so selfish. It was wonderful for Lauren and Mary to come together to help. Just as Tom and David had this morning. What would it be like to belong to that kind of family? To be cared for and supported in such a way? To simply belong...in such a way that no one could deny or take it away?

She settled into a sitting position on the edge of the bed, the tug to lie down and rest pulled at her. And nearly won. But she considered her journal, sitting on the bed table. The envelope stuck out a couple of inches at the top.

Was there a chance with Frank? Could she justify scoffing it?

Reaching for the journal, she held it to her chest. *Lord, what would you have me do?*

She didn't really expect an answer but hoped for some sense of peace. It did not come. Had God abandoned her altogether?

Gripping the letter, she freed it from the book. Now the only thing that separated her from the contents was the thin envelope. It did not create an insurmountable barrier, except in her heart.

Frank's words the last they spoke echoed in her thoughts. Had he changed his mind about her? Did she want him to? There was one way to find out.

Sliding a finger along the already torn portion of the envelope, she slid the papers out, took a breath, and unfolded them.

Why was he such a coward? Timothy had been asking himself that question for the last two hours. But was he? Or did he only try to preserve his heart, his sanity?

It wasn't as if the future was clear. He had no way of knowing what lay ahead. Though he was uncertain when it came to Jane. His heart ached for her. Yet his mind told him that the situation was not so easy. How could he consign himself to a life without family? Without children? No matter how much he loved her.

He continued to go around and around in his thoughts. Nothing resolved, no answer forthcoming.

Of all his life, he craved God's presence more now, wanted for God's direction. Where was His guiding light? His purpose? Though, had Timothy lost all hope of such when he walked away? Perhaps.

Timothy walked along the planked sidewalk. Had been for the last few hours. He told himself it was a chance to get fresh air and clear his head. But he'd only created more of a conundrum for himself. Wasn't his heart tearing him apart? If only he could find a way out of this, then he might find peace.

So, he continued walking alongside the several businesses on the main stretch of Cripple Creek. He found himself near the telegraph office. And the thought occurred to him, not for the first time: how did his former congregation fare? Had they found a replacement for him? Certainly, it couldn't be difficult to replace a preacher who had wandered far from God.

He paused. Should he send a telegram? Ask after them? He dismissed the thought almost as quickly as it came. The wondering was his due.

Turning to walk back toward the clinic, he paused and watched the stage come. It was a bit late today. Not that it was his business. Still, he waited for it to stop so he might cross the dirt road.

The stage stilled, and the driver dropped from the bench. "Cripple Creek," he hollered toward the door.

Timothy wasn't sure why he remained as he was. Curiosity maybe. Still, he needed to get back to Lemuel.

The door to the stagecoach opened and a man stepped out. He tried to get the driver's attention, but the stocky man's focus was on unloading the luggage.

So, the well-dressed man looked around, his gaze landing on Timothy.

Oh no. How did he get himself into these things?

Timothy tried to hurry as he took a step off the boardwalk.

"Sir!" the man called.

He was caught. There were two choices: ignore him like a cad or respond. The former was very tempting. But he had been coward enough for three lifetimes in these last couple of months.

"Sir," the man insisted, rushing toward Timothy.

Shifting toward the approaching figure, Timothy sighed. "Can I help you with something?"

"Yes. I am looking for Doctor..." He pulled out a slip of paper. "Sullivan. Do you know where I can find him?"

"I am actually headed to the clinic right now."

"Splendid." The man beamed. "One moment." The fine gentleman walked to the stage and grabbed for a suitcase that had just been unloaded. Then he faced Timothy again. "I'm ready."

They walked in silence for several moments. It oddly reminded him of his first encounter with Jane. Then his heart fell.

"What brings you to Cripple Creek?" Timothy asked, feeling as if he were prying, but open to a conversation that might take his mind off Jane.

"I am here to collect my fiancé." His smile widened.

Timothy felt another pang. The man's happiness was fairly oozing from him.

"Congratulations." He wanted to let that be it, but something tugged at him. "Is she a friend of Dr. Sullivan's?"

The man nodded. "His wife, actually. Are you well acquainted with the doctor?"

Timothy grunted. "It's a small town."

"Ah. I see. Perhaps you've met her then."

Timothy became more uncomfortable. And a dread came over him as the pieces started to fall into place. "Maybe. What's her name?" He asked even though, for the most part, he didn't want to know.

The man watched him, a curiosity in his affect as well. "Jane Millington."

J ane dropped down from the horse. A part of her wished she had stayed at the homestead. But she just couldn't. All the family togetherness became too hard. It fairly suffocated her.

So, she thought she might pay Lemuel a visit at the clinic. If she should happen to come across Timothy, so be it. Perhaps they may have an exchange. It wouldn't be the worst thing. In fact, it might help. She hated the way they had left things.

Though she was quite aware that he may not even want to see her.

That did little to thwart her hopes. If she could but talk to him...

Steadying herself outside the clinic door, she knocked.

"Just a moment," Wyatt's voice rang out even through the door.

Jane bit at her lip and let her heart send up whatever prayers she could.

A handful of seconds later, the door opened.

She didn't know what she reasonably expected, but she found herself face-to-face with Wyatt. And he looked both surprised and bothered.

Maybe she shouldn't have come. He did have a patient he tended to.

A whiff of familiar cologne reached her nose. She knew it from somewhere. But she hadn't known Wyatt to be fond of the stuff. Strange.

"I...am so sorry to intrude." She'd best speak her piece and return to the homestead. As dreadful as that prospect seemed.

"Is that you, Janie?" The voice was familiar, too. Though rather out of place. Both the scent and the sound collided in her memory. It couldn't be. Was that Frank?

She drew in a breath, fighting the urge to back away.

The door moved to make the opening wider and she spotted Frank beside Wyatt.

"Janie," Frank said as he pulled her past Wyatt and into the clinic. "Darling, you're here."

Stunned as she was, she couldn't make her mouth form words. He had written of his intent to pursue marriage once more, but he had not mentioned coming to Cripple Creek? What had brought this about?

"It's all right, sweetheart. I've come to take you home. Where you belong. With me." He tugged her closer, into his embrace and pressed a hard kiss to the side of her face.

She gulped. Could she push back? His grip on her was rather firm.

As her eyes adjusted to the dimmer interior, she focused on another figure farther in the room—Timothy. And he looked grim. A frown was etched into his features, and his gaze was hard. What had happened here? What had Frank divulged?

At length, she did press against Frank's chest, affording her some room. "Frank, I didn't know—"

"It's no matter. I'm here now."

"Yes," Timothy said as he glared. "Your fiancé was rather worried about you."

Fiancé? What could he mean?

Though Frank did not correct him. That was odd. She didn't remember accepting a proposal of marriage.

Wresting free of Frank's hold, she wanted to plead with Timothy. Her heart was breaking at the sight of his angry face. But was he truly angry? Or hurt?

She would wager the latter.

Timothy stepped toward the door. "Excuse me."

Wyatt moved out of his way. And for his part, seemed every bit as concerned as Jane was.

"Timothy," she blurted out after him.

But Frank grabbed for her arm again. "Aren't you glad to see me?"

"I'm...just surprised." She tried again to tug her arm free.

"Didn't you get my letter?" His insistence was maddening.

"Yes, but I..." She watched Timothy's shadow fade from beyond the door. Desperation filled her...she had to speak with him.

"You what?" Frank's voice now had an edge. Because of her lack of joy at his arrival? "I'm starting to think you didn't want me to come." The disappointment was evident in his voice.

"I...just need a minute." She threw a pleading gaze at Wyatt. Would he help her?

"Mr. Alva," Wyatt said as he stepped closer. "Let's see if we can find you a room at the boarding house."

Frank murmured something Jane couldn't discern.

Though as she tugged again, twisting her arm, she pulled free. "I'll be right back."

Then she rushed after Timothy, praying she might be able to catch him.

Jane scanned for Timothy along the street in the fading light. He was several paces toward the livery. What was going on with him? Surely, he was hurt...but did he have to keep walking away from her like this? It seemed to be his way of dealing with harder things. Was he so fragile?

"Timothy," she called as she moved toward him at the most rapid pace she could properly go with her skirt.

He kept walking. With his longer stride, it was a bit of effort to keep up, much less catch him. She found herself fairly running.

"Timothy, wait!" The words sounded desperate to her ears. But she didn't care. She was, after all, quite urgent after him.

She gained on him a bit, closing the distance. And her calls were drawing the eyes of those still about. For certain, she was making a scene. But she didn't care. He was almost to the livery. "Timothy!"

Just as she neared, he halted and spun on her.

She tried to stop before ramming into him but was only somewhat successful. Her arms flailed a bit as she tried to maintain her balance.

"What do you want, Jane?" His words were angry. But she knew better. They covered up his hurt.

"I just...need to tell you..." She fought for her breath after her race to catch him.

"What? What could you possibly need to tell me?"

She set a hand on her midsection, trying to slow her breaths so she could have this conversation. "Frank exaggerated. We are not engaged."

Timothy's expression did not alter. Did he not believe her? "No?"

She shook her head. "No. He did ask me to marry him. But I didn't say yes."

"Oh? I suppose you have to take the best offer when it comes. I thought you would be more concerned about giving up such a comfortable situation."

That stung. And why would he think such? Did he think she was so shallow? That she would marry for advantage? "I'm not. It is true that I...wanted to say yes to Frank. Planned to even. But when I told him I was..." She pushed out the word. "Barren...he said he needed time to think."

Timothy's face remained a mask of ire. Would he not soften to her plight in the least?

"I know this is not what you want to hear. But that's why I came to Cripple Creek—to give myself space to think. And I discovered that I didn't love him. Not like that."

There was a slight softening about Timothy's eyes. "Why would you say that?" His words were a touch gentler. "Isn't he everything you want?"

"Because I know what I feel for you." There, she had said it—exposing her heart to him.

As much as she wanted him to profess love for her, take her in his arms, and reissue his proposal, she didn't truly think that would happen. But she wanted—no, *needed*—for him to understand.

He pushed out a puff of air. Did he not know how to respond?

"What do you want from me?" He leaned back slightly, settling into his stance. His face was as devoid of emotion as it had been. Why wouldn't he just let her in? Even a little bit?

"I want you to tell me how you feel...what you are thinking... anything."

He sighed. "I don't know."

Didn't know what to say? Or didn't know how he felt?

She set a tentative hand to his arm. "Don't you care for me? Even a little?"

He jerked his arm away as if she had burned him. "It's not so easy as all that."

She knew that was true. But she hoped that he might push through all of it. And give her heart some assurance. That was clearly not to be.

Timothy ran a hand down his face. "I honestly don't know what to think. Or believe."

Did he not trust her enough to take her at her word? Maybe there wasn't any hope of a future here. Not anymore.

She nodded as she looked to the ground, fighting tears. "I see."

Silence thickened the space between them. How long could she hold back her emotions? Why didn't he just walk away already? He wanted to. She could sense as much.

"I..." he started but paused.

Something sparked in her...might his next words be a balm to her wounded heart?

He cleared his throat. "I need to get Lemuel to the house. He is probably worn out with the day."

His words sliced through her. She couldn't hardly catch her breath. There wasn't anything here to salvage. "All right."

He turned to the livery but only took a step before pausing. Would he take it all back?

"He's probably at the clinic," Timothy muttered. Then stepped around her and walked back the way he had come.

She trembled...the swell of emotion so great. But she couldn't fall apart here in the middle of the street with all these people staring. Even so, she did.

Timothy was fairly shaking when he made it back to the clinic. What had he done? How could he hurt Jane like that? But he had to. He wasn't about to find himself the odd man out again if she opted to stay with Frank. He didn't think his heart could bear a second rejection. Not when he cared so deeply. Perhaps more than he ever had for Katherine.

He pushed the door open and found himself in an empty exam room. Where had Wyatt and Frank gone? Oh yes, Wyatt had promised to help Frank get a room at the boarding house. How long would they be gone? Timothy didn't feel right about leaving with Lemuel without Wyatt here.

They decided it might be better for Lemuel to go to Timothy's house for the night. The clinic was no place for him. Certainly not with his pa in the other room suffering. Where was the boy?

Timothy made his way to the back of the clinic and up the stairs to the recovery rooms. The one Lemuel had stayed in last night was vacant. His stomach lurched. Had something happened to the boy? Had he run off?

166

Then he heard it—Lemuel's voice. The door to Mr. Langley's room was cracked just a bit. Timothy spotted the lad within, sitting by his father's bed.

Straining, Timothy tried to pick up what was happening without disrupting him.

"I know Pa ain't always been the best. He sure does have a heap of guilt on him. But help him get better, God. I don't want him to die."

Timothy jerked back at the words of the prayer. How could the boy want God to heal and return his father to him? A man that beat on him and probably tossed angry words his way. What kind of grace and faith did this boy have?

Lemuel had not displayed the best behavior in their early interactions, but that didn't mean he lacked faith, clearly. Perhaps the boy was hurting from not having his ma the same as Mr. Langley was. Maybe more, as he didn't have a pa to turn to either.

Timothy's heart went out to the boy. And he found himself looking heavenward. He would pray if he thought there was a real chance God would hear him. But he'd already crossed a bridge that left him cut off from the Almighty. Hadn't he?

Yet the truth of Scriptures learned long ago whispered in his heart. Was it true that God would never leave nor forsake him? The Bible said so, but it didn't seem right. Not after the way Timothy had walked away...rather, he ran from his calling. What did he lean into—what his brain told him about reasonable behavior or what the Bible said about God?

He backed farther from the door as Lemuel continued his child-like prayer. And he slipped into the vacated room. Then he looked to the ceiling, imagining he could see much farther than the wooden boards.

What will it be, God? Are You listening? I've made a mess of everything I've touched. Maybe because I relied on myself, on my own understanding. Even when I was in the pulpit.

It was true. Timothy had always had a great sense of things. And had counted on that to get him through situations. Then it ran out. He had been wrong about Katherine, and it had shaken him. Hard. So hard that he couldn't playact anymore. Then he was lost.

But was he? Or was he the one keeping himself from a real relationship with Jesus? Could he turn his life over? Lean on God for his future?

Footfalls on the stairs disrupted his thoughts. Who was in the clinic? He stepped into the hall in time to see Wyatt coming from the steps.

He nodded at the man who had become more friend than foe of late.

"I saw Jane outside." Wyatt's words were simple. Almost biting.

Timothy nodded and looked toward the recovery room with Mr. Langley and Lemuel. "Can we not talk about it?"

The blue of Wyatt's eyes became steely.

"At least...not here." Timothy indicated the room behind Wyatt.

Wyatt held up a hand for Timothy to return below stairs.

As they came into the main clinic area, Timothy let out a breath and turned. "I know what you think, but it's not your concern."

Wyatt appeared as if he were about to speak but stopped himself. He seemed to consider his next words, then spoke. "You're right."

Timothy let out a breath. At least he wouldn't have to have a pointless exchange with Wyatt. An exchange which no doubt would make him feel more guilty and regret his actions, regardless of how justified he felt.

Wyatt continued. "Mr. Langley is steadily improving, however slowly. But I think he will recover in time."

"And what of Lemuel?"

Wyatt's gaze softened. "You know we can't do anything but let him go back home with his pa. As much as I want to protect him...as much as I would if I were certain about what went on in that house. But I can't just go taking children from their parents. Even if the law allowed it."

Timothy frowned. "I can't say I blame you."

Wyatt's stance eased and his shoulders dropped a little. Had he been prepared for a confrontation?

Timothy moved toward the stairs again to collect Lemuel. "Actually, I can."

"What?" The question in Wyatt's eyes was sincere.

"I can blame you."

Wyatt's brows furrowed.

"You know very well what it is to live in such a situation. Why would you not do anything and everything you could to keep Lemuel safe?"

Wyatt seethed. "It's not that I don't care. Or want to help Lemuel. But I haven't seen anything beyond a limp that makes me suspicious. And that can be explained away easily. I talked to him and there was no indication that anything untoward was happening."

Timothy's hands curled into fists. He wanted to hit something. The wall, the door...anything that might harmlessly take the brunt of his frustration. "Would *you* have told someone about your pa? Did you?"

"Don't get all irate," Wyatt said, stepping toward him. "Why don't you take Lemuel home, and we'll revisit this tomorrow. If you want, try to talk to him. Maybe that will ease your suspicions."

Timothy narrowed his gaze. But he couldn't begrudge Wyatt's sense in the matter. So, he nodded.

"Let me collect him and check on Mr. Langley." Wyatt maneuvered around Timothy and to the stairs.

Timothy was left with his built-up anger. He would find a way to keep Lemuel safe. Even if he had to kidnap the boy and start fresh somewhere else.

Jane barely noticed as her body rocked in the wagon. She sat beside Wyatt and tried desperately to contain her emotions. They had bid Frank farewell with a promise to collect him the next day after school. Once Frank had her alone, he would insist they leave for San Francisco as soon as possible. Is that what she wanted?

What would it be like to marry Frank? He was solid, dependable, and made enough money to keep her comfortable. He must have decided that children weren't as important as he had initially thought. It was, in the end, a good offer for her situation. Were matches best made for such reasons? Love aside, it was a wise choice. And marriages across the ages had been made primarily for more sensible reasons than love.

"You seem pretty lost in thought." Wyatt's words peeled her away from her rambling mind.

"I'm sorry I'm not very good company tonight." The guilt needled at her. Wyatt and Kitty had been so good to her. Overly generous. But she couldn't live off friends and connections for the rest of her life.

"It's all right. I was just...wondering." Wyatt kept his gaze pinned on the horse in front of them.

"Oh?" What could have him so diverted?

"You're important to Katie. And you've helped out in more ways than I'll ever be able to thank you."

That was gracious of him to say, even more gracious than she deserved. They had given her a safe place and kindness. It was she who owed them a great thanks.

"I have my wife back. Who knows how bad things could have gotten had I continued to ignore—"

"You don't have to do that." Jane's words were rather quiet. She had no desire to revisit the hard things they had faced with Kat.

Wyatt looked at her. "I just don't want you to think you have to go anywhere or do anything. You'll always have a place with us."

She looked away so he wouldn't see her tears. Again, that was a kindness extended, but she dared not take advantage of it. No, it was best she make a life for herself. If that meant she needed to marry Frank, then so be it. She may not love him, but he was a decent man who cared about her. But she didn't think it prudent to share all of that with Wyatt. "I appreciate that."

He nodded as he jerked the reins, directing the animal northward. "Just want you to know that you're not alone."

But there was no escaping the simple fact, the truth that stared back at her in the mirror: she was alone...so very alone.

CHAPTER 16

Faith Long Lost

Timothy had no idea why he was here. But he stared at the pulpit of the church, eyeing the altar as well. So much of his energy and time had been spent in these very places. Did he ever have a passion, a fire after God's word? A strong desire to teach it to others? Yes. He knew as much was true.

Then what had happened? To him? To his calling? To his dedication?

Katherine.

But no, it wasn't just her. And Wyatt wasn't to blame either. Timothy had managed his own way into that situation. Then his actions took it a step further when he tried to convince Katherine to annul her marriage. Even now his face heated from the memory.

If no one else was to blame, then he would have to face the truth: Katherine didn't love him. Never did. Oh, she cared for him, he was certain. But not the way she cared for Wyatt. Ever.

How could he not have seen it sooner?

But this, he knew as well—he hadn't wanted to, so he didn't.

All this time, he had tried to push that burden anywhere but on his own shoulders, but that's where it squarely belonged.

The door creaked and he turned, letting his eyes confirm who he knew it to be—Reverend Dawson.

"Oh, Mr. Johnson." The man sounded genuinely surprised to see him in the church. Had he stayed away so long? Had the man an inkling how far Timothy had wandered?

"Good day, Reverend." The word felt strange even now. Yes, Reverend Dawson earned that title, but a part of Timothy ached for it to be his again.

That surprised. Why would he wish such? Was it simply his desire to have a place? Or was there something deeper in the aching of his heart?

"Can I help you with something?" The man's voice softened. As if he knew.

And Timothy wondered...what, in fact, did the man know?

"I'm just...thinking."

"This is a fine place to do that." Reverend Dawson sat on the pew across the aisle from Timothy's position. "Always has been."

Timothy watched the man as he closed his eyes. His lips moved as well...as if he prayed even then. Not wishing to disrupt him, Timothy turned his attention back to the cross at the front of the room.

He had never felt so much the sinner as he did now...after his heart had fallen far from God, from His will.

"Anything you care to share in those thoughts?"

Timothy turned to see the reverend's gaze intent on him.

"I've been told I'm a good listener." The man smiled at that, then chuckled. "Except for my wife. She would tell you an entirely different story."

Timothy couldn't help but return the smile. The man really was easy to be around. Perhaps he would be good to talk to. "I've been asking myself—where do I belong?"

"Hmmm," the man muttered. "I think that's a good question."

"I believed at one time very much that serving God was where I had been called. Then I didn't."

"Well, I know when life gets rough, things can get shaky in the faith department."

Timothy nodded. Was that all? "But aren't preachers and Biblical teachers expected to know better?"

"You know as well as I do that whether that's true or not in peoples' minds, that we are just as human and fallible as anyone else. Maybe more so. We may not put ourselves in the same tempting situations as other men, but we can be tempted in other ways."

That was certainly true.

"In my younger years," Reverend Dawson continued, "I thought I had all the answers. God had called me to be a preacher, so I needed to, right?"

Timothy couldn't help but watch the man as he made himself vulnerable.

"I don't have the same great testimony as some...being rescued from a life of carousing, gambling, and drinking too much. I was simply always dedicated to God's plan."

Timothy couldn't help but think that his own story was being told.

"It took a while for me to realize that I still had my own selfish pride to deal with. And it may be harder to see self-righteousness though it plagues the heart just the same."

Timothy nodded again, not trusting himself to say anything.

"I may not be the prodigal. But I have been the older brother."

Such truth. Timothy knew it was his story too...at least in part. How often had he thought himself, even only in his heart, better off because he didn't sin the same? How often had he dismissed his own sins of complacency and self-reliance? How many times had he judged others instead of looking at the fallacies in his own heart?

"I...think I needed to hear that," he said to the reverend. "Thank you."

The older man gave him a meaningful look. Then, after some moments of silence, he rose. "I think I'll let you alone to do that thinking."

As the preacher exited, Timothy found himself with no reason to prolong this uncomfortable silence. But when he thought about leaving, it didn't settle well either. Years ago, he would have counseled someone that this was evidence of the Holy Spirit tugging at their heart. Was that the case?

He set his gaze on the cross again and wondered.

The prodigal was never unwelcomed by his father, no matter how far he had gone, or what sin had darkened his heart. And Timothy knew. It was time to go home.

Jane settled into the chair Frank had pulled out for her. The bustle of the café surrounded them. And it comforted her torn heart somewhat, being surrounded by townsfolk enjoying their supper.

"There." Frank scooted the chair closer to the table before he took his seat.

Jane watched him. He was a good man, if maybe a little self-focused. But he did care for her. Perhaps more than she deserved.

"That smells delicious," he commented as he arranged his eating utensils, lining them up impossibly straighter. Was he nervous?

They had not yet had the chance to be alone together to discuss... anything. Did he still fancy them engaged? She had not corrected him. Yet.

Her heart was not at home with him. But was there truly anything to hope for with Timothy? It seemed doubtful.

"You are quiet." Frank leaned forward, intent on her.

"I am thinking about the children."

"Oh?" Frank spoke dismissively. Did he not think she should bother? "Well, they won't be your concern in a couple of days. And you won't have to worry with teaching ever again." He smiled as if this option was everything she could want.

It wasn't. Jane enjoyed teaching. And making a difference. Especially since...she would never have her own children to dote on. But how could she make him understand that?

"Where are the menus?" He glanced about the room.

She chuckled at that. "There aren't any. This isn't like the restaurants you're used to. We have two choices. That's it. No need for a menu."

"How...quaint," he muttered. Then he shot her a smile. "It will be nice to be back home, don't you think?"

A thickness in her throat kept her from answering. So, she nodded, hesitantly.

"I purchased us passage back to San Francisco on Saturday." He beamed as if he offered her the crown of England.

"So soon?" She wouldn't have much time then. If she intended to go with him. But had she any other real option? Sure, Kitty and Wyatt would let her stay, but that wasn't something she wanted to entertain long term. Maybe this was her best path forward.

"I thought you might be excited to get home. And I need to get back to my business. I cannot tarry here much longer."

It was a bit of a surprise, but if she were to make her future with Frank, it had best be sooner rather than later. "Yes, I suppose."

Though she couldn't help the forlorn feeling that gripped her heart. It would be difficult to say farewell to Kitty and Wyatt. And their children. But it must be done.

Maybe she could stay...even just a little longer. She opened her mouth to suggest that very thing when Mrs. Abby strode to the table.

"Welcome, folks." She filled their water glasses. "We have meatloaf and beef stew tonight. What can I get for you?" She had a businesslike air about herself. The café was rather full already. Perhaps she was only distracted.

Jane looked up. "The meatloaf smells amazing. I'll have that."

Frank cringed slightly. Almost too quick to catch it. "The beef stew, please."

"And some tea," Jane added with an encouraging smile.

"Anything else for you?" Mrs. Abby turned to Frank.

"Coffee," he said, then shifted his focus back to Jane, all but dismissing the woman.

But Mrs. Abby didn't seem to mind. She nodded and moved off.

Frank reached out, palm up, fingers extended...waiting for Jane to set her hand in his.

She hesitated but did so.

He squeezed her fingers. "Shall we talk about the wedding arrangements?"

She squirmed. Hopefully it wasn't obvious. "Can we wait until we get to San Francisco?" Why was she saying that? Had she already decided to go with him? To marry him? Something tugged at her, anchoring her here. But she had already been through all that, hadn't she? Should she risk a solid future with Frank for the chance Timothy might change his mind? He seemed well steeped in his own challenges right now. Not that she could blame him. He had lost his mother and taken in a troubled boy.

But bless it all, she loved him.

"What is it?" Frank's words broke into her thoughts.

She shook her head. "Perhaps I am a bit tired."

Mrs. Abby came by with their hot beverages then left again.

He nodded. "I see. Well, my mother will want to hurry things along when we get back."

"Your mother will what?"

"The wedding. Jane, honestly, are you listening at all?"

She pressed his palm. "I apologize, Frank. I am rather distracted this evening."

"I don't like seeing you so concerned." He pulled her hand closer, causing her to lean in.

"Frank, I'm not sure that..." Her voice trailed as Timothy walked into the café.

Her cheeks heated, and she couldn't tear her eyes from him.

He looked about the room. Did he seek someone out? Or look for a place to sit? How could she bear it if he remained for supper?

His gaze caught hers and he jerked a little. Was he just surprised? Or upset?

But as she let her gaze rest in his, she did not discern any ire. Rather, he seemed saddened. Because she was with Frank? Because it seemed she had made a decision? Hadn't she?

Timothy lingered in the moment but then turned and walked out.

Jane's breath caught.

"What is it, darling?" Frank's words were steeped in concern.

"Nothing." She was numbed by Timothy's easy dismissal. Had he decided that whatever had been between them was over? Would he not ask her to stay?

But she knew he wouldn't. His heart wasn't available after all. There was no use in wishing for something that would never be.

Turning to Frank, she pressed a smile onto her features. "I don't need a big wedding. Let's just go to the preacher and get it done."

Frank lifted an eyebrow. "Is that really what you want? I always thought women needed a big show."

"Not me. I just want us to start our life together."

His concern melted into a smile. "Then that's what we'll do."

Timothy walked into the clinic. He still hadn't shaken the image of Jane in the café yesterday from his mind. Or heart. She looked so lost. But she had been eating with Frank. Maybe it was for the best that she turn her heart in that direction.

Wyatt looked up as Timothy closed the door.

"How is Mr. Langley?" Timothy pushed the question out. He was concerned still about Lemuel having to return to his pa. It left an unsettled weight in the pit of his stomach.

"He is much better. In fact, I think he'll be able to go home day after tomorrow."

"Saturday?" So soon? The anchor became heavier.

Wyatt nodded and continued cleaning his instruments. Timothy had noticed that Wyatt did so regularly when there were extra moments to spare. Probably a good idea.

"Do you want to see him?" Wyatt watched Timothy closely.

Timothy balked. Should he speak with Mr. Langley? Would such a conversation go well? "No. I just...wondered."

Wyatt's eyebrow lifted. "How are things coming along at the schoolhouse?"

Timothy frowned, and guilt pressed against his heart. "I haven't been involved in the repairs since..." He couldn't bring himself to speak of his mother's passing. It was still too fresh.

Wyatt focused on his cutting instruments. "I had heard that Tom and David decided to help. I just didn't realize that they weren't assisting."

Timothy shrugged. "It's probably better."

Wyatt looked at him. "Oh?"

What was Wyatt insinuating? Did he think Timothy was a coward for avoiding Jane? So be it. Timothy was only doing what he needed to preserve his heart. There was no point in chasing that thought. Maybe he'd best change the subject. "I suppose I'll bring Lemuel by tomorrow after school."

"Sure." Wyatt laid the sharp-edged implement down and picked up something that looked like pliers.

Timothy tipped his head and turned toward the door.

"Jane came home with news last night." Wyatt's words smacked Timothy square in the chest, and he paused.

"She did?" He could hardly swallow past the lump that had formed in his throat.

"Yep. She's headed to San Francisco come Saturday."

So soon? Timothy looked back at Wyatt. "Why are you telling me this?"

"Just thought you might like to know." Wyatt turned his attention to his work again.

Timothy couldn't move. He didn't know what to think. But...

maybe it would be better if she moved on. Then he could start to heal. He had just found his footing in the spiritual realm. He couldn't manage this, too. Not when the very thought made his chest feel as if it were caving in.

As Timothy opened the door, Wyatt spoke again. "She says they will get married soon after they get back."

What should that matter to Timothy? Why did Wyatt torture him with this information? But he paused and thought better on his response.

Lord, what am I to do? I don't want this to happen. But what can I do? She's made up her mind.

Timothy settled into his prayer. And worked to surrender his heart's desire to the Lord. It was difficult, but, then again, he was quite out of practice. Though he did believe God's will was best. He had to hold to that firmly if he ever planned to have a life rooted in God's way, whatever that might be.

Wyatt put the medical tool down and watched him, as if waiting for something.

"Tell her I wish her all the best." Timothy pushed the words out before exiting and pulling the door closed. He must deny his emotions in consideration for her choice. Wasn't that how God had treated him? Allowed him to make his own choices...no matter how they strayed from God's will.

Besides, hadn't he made up his mind as well when he walked away for the hundredth time? She didn't deserve that. She deserved every happiness in life. And he would not stand in her way.

CHAPTER 17

Endings

J ane was rather proud of herself. She had not broken down once the entire day—her last day with the children. *Stop,* she admonished herself. She could do this.

Gazing out at the young faces, hard at work on their arithmetic lesson, she took a moment—only a moment—to bemoan her situation. She had come to love these children. And wished very much that she could stay. There was no denying that. But it wasn't possible.

Would she stay here—regardless of Timothy's choice—if she could have secured the teaching position? She didn't know. And didn't want to think on it.

Everything had been done to make ready the schoolhouse for the new teacher. The floor and roof had been repaired and the wood stove fixed. The mildew smell had been replaced with the scent of fresh pine.

Shaking her head to clear it, Jane looked at the watch pinned near her collar.

"Let's put our slates away," she announced. There wasn't much time left in the school day. And she couldn't send them off without telling them how she felt. Pushing out a breath, she settled herself. This would not be easy.

There was a rustle of movement as the children obeyed. Then their eyes were on her again.

"I...have something to tell you all," she started.

A few eyes widened, and some, especially the older students, appeared as if they already knew. Jessie and Jack offered small smiles, while Peter looked distracted.

"There's no easy way to say this, because I have come to appreciate and care for each of you..." She let her gaze sweep the room, landing on each student. My, how she cared. "But I—"

She was interrupted by a knock on the back door.

Jane furrowed her brow. Who would be disrupting the school day? "Just a minute," she called out as she moved in that direction.

But it was as if she hadn't spoken, for the door opened and Mayor Jacobson walked in, a young woman trailing behind. This wasn't the new teacher, was it? The mayor wouldn't bring her here while Jane was saying her farewells, would he?

"Hello, Miss Millington, children," the mayor said as he ushered the woman to the front of the room.

He wouldn't. He wouldn't take this moment, this opportunity from her, would he? How would it seem if she herself didn't tell the children?

"Mayor, if I may—"

"Don't worry, Miss Millington, this will only take a few moments.

Her heart dropped.

"Children," he said as he set a hand to the young woman's shoulder.

The woman beamed at the students.

"This is Miss Virginia Newham. Your new teacher."

There was a sputtering of gasps and other disgruntled noises from the children. And Jane could have sunk through the floor.

"Well, let's give Miss Newham a warm welcome," Mayor Jacobson encouraged the students.

Jane stepped forward and waved a hand for the class to say in unison with her, "Hello, Miss Newham."

"Thank you," the younger woman said. "I am so excited to be a part of your learning journey. And I want to thank Miss Mullingson for taking such good care of you all."

Jane wanted to correct her, but what was the point? She would be a distant memory soon enough. What did it matter if the woman couldn't say her name right?

"Children, please form a line to come and meet Miss Newham." The mayor lifted an arm in the direction he expected them to come.

It seemed everything had become about Miss Newham. Was there a place for Jane anymore? Even to say her farewells?

No. Even that had been taken from her.

The children formed a line and, one by one, introduced themselves to Miss Newham. They tossed looks at Jane, but for all intents and purposes, she had been relegated to the side, all but forgotten. At least the children seemed to care. But would she remain in their minds after she had departed?

A wave of grief overcame her, and she leaned against her desk for support. After holding herself together for the entire week, for this long day, she couldn't hold the tears back anymore. She made certain to dab them with her handkerchief and to not make a sound.

Perhaps her sorrow would escape anyone's notice.

Timothy shifted yet again. Sleep just would not come to him tonight. Was his mind so clouded? For here, in the quiet of his room, in the dark of the night—and only here—he allowed himself to think on Jane. And the fact that she would be leaving on the stage tomorrow.

But only for a few moments. He didn't have the capacity to take on the whole of his sadness at the way things had turned out. Though, as he kept telling himself, it was for the best. He had been broken. And only now did he allow God to put him back together. This was no space to bring a fine woman into. No, she should be with someone whole.

Frank seemed to have himself settled. That was what she needed. Perhaps, even, what she wanted.

Timothy stared out the window at the bright moon making its journey across the night sky. It was especially luminating tonight, cutting through the dark as if nothing would stand in his way.

If only he could see his path as clearly as he could the things in the path of the moonbeams. If only he could be so bold.

But there was no going back. No changing his mind. That would not solve anything. He needed to let Jane go…in life as well as in his heart.

Who knew? Maybe God had a plan in this…bringing him through this hard place to prepare him for what came next. Perhaps God had a life of solitude in mind for him. Hadn't the apostle Paul preached about serving God single-mindedly? Or maybe there was another woman in his future. Though he doubted he would ever love so much again. Despite his best attempts not to, he cared so very deeply for her.

Perhaps rescuing Lemuel from his situation was God's purpose. Then Timothy might be absolved. For the church he had left, as he understood, had not been able to find another preacher. If only he could step back into the pulpit. But it was too soon and his healing too new.

Tomorrow, Mr. Langley would go home. And probably would resume drinking and expressing his anger and grief the way he had been.

Why couldn't Wyatt care more? Was Timothy the only one who saw the boy's timid nature underneath the brazen rulebreaker? Or the injuries to his person? For certain, Timothy had spotted bruises just under the boy's shirt collar. It was too hard to stomach.

God, what would You have me do? Would it be wrong to take the boy somewhere safe? You permitted the Egyptian midwives to defy authority to save the Hebrew babies...and Moses. That had been a part of Your plan. Maybe it's time I did some defying of this unjust way.

He continued to pray, but his weariness caught up with him. As it did so, a peace settled over him. Sleep would come, then.

A loud *thud* stirred him back to full awareness. *What was that?*

He sat up, straining to hear what had disrupted him from drifting off.

There it was again—this time more of a *thump thump*.

He slid from the bed and moved to the great room. Was someone outside? Maneuvering toward the door, he was redirected when the sound recommenced. It wasn't coming from the direction of the front door, but from the room Lemuel was in.

Was the boy trying to escape into the night? Afraid to return to his pa's care?

Timothy rushed to the small room and jerked the door open. Then he sucked in a breath at what he found.

Lemuel was not at the window, but on the floor. Convulsing.

Timothy rushed to steady him. What was happening here? It seemed like some kind of fit. The boy shook and jerked but did not seem alert.

"Lemuel," he said, pressing a hand to the lad's chest, trying to still the boy. "Lemuel."

There was no response.

Timothy watched, helpless to do anything. Should he go for Wyatt? Or was this something spiritual? He did not know.

God, help this child, show me how.

As quickly as the tremors seemed to come upon the boy, they stopped. And Lemuel lay in what appeared to be a deep sleep.

Timothy lifted him back into the bed and covered him up. But he remained in the room for quite some time, ensuring that all was indeed well.

And Timothy had a thought: was this something that happened often? Not just a one-night occurrence? If so, such attacks could certainly lead to bruises and other injuries. That would mean, however, that everything Timothy relied on to support Mr. Langley's abuse was not valid.

Could he be wrong? And, if so, what else was he wrong about?

Jane held onto Kitty as they watched the luggage being loaded. She wasn't certain she could stand on her own if she didn't have her friend to lean on.

The last few hours had been torture. She said her farewells to the children and to Tom and Lauren as they came to watch the little ones, so Kitty and Wyatt were able to be with her now.

She wasn't sure what she would do—would have done this whole time—without their support. But thankfully, she didn't have to know. Because she had them beside her. For at least the next several minutes. Kitty would be here to see her off. Then she would be on her own.

No, not on her own...with Frank, her husband-to-be. She would have someone to care for her and keep her. That was good, right, and true.

If that were so, then why did her heart ache and tear at her for her choice?

It wasn't as if she didn't know. She cared for Timothy. So much it hurt. And even more because her affection was not returned. Not in any depth that mattered.

Still, she watched the edge of town, wishing and hoping for him to come riding in to rescue her from this life she had settled for. Again, she chastised herself. It was more than that. She had never belonged with anyone. And now she would. Timothy had not offered her that. But Frank did. That's what mattered, right?

The last of the bags were being loaded. Frank and Wyatt chatted a few steps away as they supervised the men working. Their conversation was adamant, but Jane couldn't hear it.

"I will miss you terribly." Kitty dabbed at her eyes with her handkerchief. "You've been a godsend."

Jane embraced her friend, wishing she could hold to her much longer than the few moments she did. "I will miss you!"

"Don't think you can't visit, though." Kitty patted her back gently.

Then they separated. Jane wished she could tell Kitty that it would happen. But Frank had not been so fond of this place. She truly doubted it would be an option.

"Same to you. And I'm not the only one who would love to see you visit San Francisco." Jane kept her words measured to keep from begging. That would not be suitable.

Kitty nodded, but they both knew this might very well be their final farewell.

Jane intended to write. Nothing could stop her from that. But, as much as it would be unlikely for her to convince Frank to visit again, she knew that Wyatt's ability to travel was limited. The people of Cripple Creek needed their doctor. And Kitty would not be apt to take the children or be separated from them for so long.

The thought of not seeing Kitty again deepened Jane's grief at leaving. Did it have to be so hard?

Frank turned back toward Jane. "You ready, darling?"

She wasn't. Not even a little bit. But she must press into her future.

He held out a hand for her and she squeezed Kitty once more before slipping her fingers onto his. His grip held her fast and tugged her toward himself.

"The best is yet to come," he said softly, the words forming a promise.

It did nothing to ease her apprehension. Still, she nodded.

He pressed a kiss to the side of her face.

She allowed it. There would be no sense in denying him affection.

But as she turned her head to accept it, she focused once more in the direction of Timothy's home. Nothing. Not even the stirring of dirt.

As he pulled back, Frank urged her to the stagecoach.

Jane looked back toward Kat, now with Wyatt beside her. "Thank you...for everything." Her words were choked and thick with emotion. She would miss these people. They had become dear to her. And, while she had been asked to help them, they had really given her a place to belong. If only for a little while.

Kitty nodded, not doing anything to stop her own tears as she held to her husband.

Then Jane let Frank lead her to the stage. But as he opened the door, she heard a small voice that seemed to be farther away.

"Wait! Stop!"

She paused and looked in the direction of the sound. Was it Timothy? No, it was much too young. Her face heated at her girlish sentiments.

Frank let out a long breath. It seemed as if he were exasperated.

Scanning the area, she was surprised to see Jack running at them. Wasn't he supposed to be at the homestead with his grandparents?

Soon enough, several smaller feet thundered on the ground. It was the school children. Coming her way. They were the brightest sight she could have hoped for, filling the street in a wave of love as they marched in their uneven way.

Jack stopped just short of the stagecoach. "Miss Millington..." He turned and waited as the others neared. With them were Lauren and Tom. Somehow, they had been involved. For certain.

Shifting her focus to the lad in front of her she asked, "What is it, Jack? What's going on?"

"We need to go, Janie," Frank insisted.

She put a hand to his arm. "Just a minute." Then she focused on Jack. "What's all this about?"

The rest of the class had reached the telegraph office and stood on the planked sidewalk, watching her.

"We wanted to see you off," Jack's face seemed to redden as he spoke.

Jessie stepped forward. "We hope you know we love you and will miss you."

Jane set a hand to her heart, which was racing and, with each beat, grew. She had thought...maybe a bit...that the children hadn't cared if she stayed or went. And the way the last school day had gone, her doubt had deepened.

The mayor came out from behind the children. When had he shown up? "This town owes you a great debt, Miss Millington. Even though you were only here for a couple of months, you have carved out a place in our hearts. We wish you all the best, but you will be missed."

Jane wanted to cry. In fact, she had to press her hand to her lips to keep from doing just that. She was loved, appreciated, needed, and wanted. Surely, she would burst with such overwhelming gratitude.

Stepping around Frank, whose smile was definitely not genuine, Jane pulled Jessie and Jack to herself. The other children clamored in to join the embrace.

"Why are you crying?" Peter asked. "Are you sad?"

Jane flapped her hands to cool her face and calm herself. "No, dear, not at all. I'm very, very happy."

The small boy beamed.

She wished she could wrap these children up and take this feeling with her always. And she would...she would treasure this moment forever.

Frank hooked her elbow. "The driver says he has to leave now. He has a schedule to keep."

She nodded, knowing it was true, yet reluctant to do so. "I will take you with me. Each of you. And remember your kindnesses toward me."

The children pressed in again.

But Mayor Jacobson stepped between them and Jane, shoeing them a safe distance from the stagecoach.

Frank pulled Jane to the door and onto the bench, putting himself between her and the exterior window facing the children.

She leaned forward, looking around him, and blew kisses to the children.

"Lean back," he all but commanded. "This thing is pretty shaky."

She didn't care.

When the stage jerked into motion, Frank held to her to keep her from falling off the bench. But she kept her gaze on the surrogate family she'd had until the town was only a strip on the horizon. It was then that she settled back and closed her eyes, relishing the love expressed toward her.

And in that moment, she realized...Timothy had not come.

CHAPTER 18

Realizations

Timothy shuffled into the clinic. It had been a long day. A long, very emotional day. And he was tired of fighting it. But he had to.

He had seen Jane leave from his position within the General Store. He couldn't stay away. There had been little he could do to stop himself from seeing her one last time. Though it had been difficult to restrain himself. Something just felt wrong about watching her ride off.

But it had warmed his heart that the children gave her such a grand send-off. Of anyone in town, she had earned it, devoting herself tirelessly amid her own struggles.

Now, he trudged about as if his feet weighed a hundred pounds each. He wanted to shut the world out and languish in his home. But he couldn't. Not with this discovery of Lemuel's episodes. A conversation with Wyatt was forthcoming. And he would not shy away from it.

Now that Timothy looked about the clinic's exam room, he wasn't sure where Wyatt could have gone. The space was empty, save the medical equipment and whatnot. No doctor there to greet him.

"Doc?" he called out, unsure why he would address his old friend as such. That's what the people in this town called him though.

Someone came down the back stairs. He heard the gentle *thump thump* of feet on the steps. Then Wyatt emerged, his features registering his surprise when he met Timothy's gaze. "Timothy?"

"Ah. I wondered where you were. I trust Mr. Langley is still doing well."

Wyatt nodded then crossed his arms. "But I'm not so sure where *your* mind is."

The words had been harsh. More so than he'd expected. What had Timothy done now?

"Excuse me?" Something in Timothy riled at Wyatt's tone, but he forced his words to remain even and calm. Nothing would be gained by letting his own insecurities control his behavior.

"I don't understand you." Wyatt shook his head, raising his hands as if in frustration. "You let her go? You just stood by and let her leave?"

Timothy felt the warmth drain from his face. As if this hadn't been hard enough without someone throwing it in his face. "I...was only doing what is best for her."

Wyatt scoffed. "You know better. She watched for you, waited for you, needed you to come stop her from making a mistake."

"I don't think this is any of your business," Timothy said, his words kept soft, a difficult thing with the war inside himself. But he kept a genial tone.

"Well, I'm making it my business." Wyatt's tone, however, was raised. "How could you let your only real chance for happiness just ride off?"

"I..." What were his reasons again? He had them. And they were good reasons. Ah, yes, she deserved more, and he was still uncertain what God had for his future. "I can't be what she needs."

"Pshhh," Wyatt released on a hissed breath. "You're afraid."

Timothy's eyes widened. That wasn't true.

"You let what happened between all of us affect you to such an extent that you let the woman you love leave town. Forever." Wyatt shook his head. "I don't know what else to say."

Timothy would be fine if Wyatt stopped talking altogether.

But Wyatt let out a tense breath and went on. "But I see now that the past has continued to plague you. And…" He paused and looked toward the ceiling. Was he beseeching God now? "I would like your forgiveness."

What? Hadn't Timothy come to a place where he accepted it wasn't anyone's fault but his? Though he couldn't deny the swirl of emotion, the pang, at Wyatt's entreaty.

"I…"

"Please, Timothy, let's forgive each other and put this behind us. If for no other reason than so you can live life again."

Timothy nodded but didn't trust himself to speak. What could he say? He fought too hard to contain the swell within himself.

Wyatt released a breath that saw his shoulders ease and the muscles in his jaw relax. "Thank you."

They stood in silence. Timothy struggled against a nagging in the back of his mind. What was that?

"Wow." Wyatt crossed his arms and looked to the floor, then at Timothy. "I didn't realize how much I needed that."

Timothy's eyebrows rose. Had Wyatt carried a burden as well? But the heaviness that had been Timothy's constant companion these last years lifted. He felt free. Was this what God had been trying to show him all along? Forgiveness had been the answer.

Yet he still ached, pain throbbing with each heartbeat. Had he not truly forgiven Wyatt and Katherine? No, he knew he had. A peace washed over him that was like no other. Though a wound remained all the same.

"Let me speak as your friend." Wyatt's words were direct. "I don't know what's happened with you and how your life has been since…for the last couple of years. But I know this: you won't be right until you tell her how you feel."

"I don't know if I—"

"No matter what she says..." Wyatt slashed an arm through the air. "Whether she stays or goes...you need to tell her all of it. Trust me on this." Wyatt's eyes radiated a sincere concern. For Timothy? Or for Jane? Or...what did it matter anyway? He was right.

Timothy sucked in a breath as the full force of his affection for Jane overwhelmed him. He did love her. So very much.

How could he have let her go?

"You're right. I...have to go after her." Timothy rushed for the door.

"They're headed for Victor."

Timothy paused and nodded at Wyatt. "Thanks. And...I need your forgiveness, too. I—"

"It's already been given." Wyatt waved his hands toward the door. "Go! Before it's too late!"

Timothy bolted out the door and rushed for his horse. Everything homed in on this one purpose, this one mission. He had to bring her back. Or at least try.

Lord, give me success. Be with me.

The few words were all he could think to pray as he untied his horse from the post and mounted. Then he was off.

Most of the ride to Victor was spent in silence. And Jane wondered what went on in Frank's mind. Still, she could not bring herself to ask him...that or anything else. Though she felt so warmed by the sendoff from Cripple Creek, she didn't quite have the nerve to face the future. Or her future husband. So, she gripped the bench and tried to steady herself against the bumping of the stagecoach.

"Are you comfortable?" he looked up from his book and asked. It felt a bit forced.

"Not really," she said, believing there not benefit to falsehoods. "I'm quite uneasy with all this movement." And her stomach churned, but she'd best not mention that. It seemed a bit unladylike.

"Perhaps a short walk in Victor will suit you. We won't be there long, but I can insist we be permitted that much."

She offered a half-hearted smile. "Thank you."

He turned back to his book, but she watched him, wondering after their life together. Frank was a good man. Decent at the very least. Maybe a bit more involved in himself and his job. That had always been a challenge for them.

And, for as long as they had courted, there wasn't the rush of emotion when he looked at her. Or the racing of her heart when they touched. But those were not the things to base a marriage on, right? Besides, she wasn't sure she put much stock in God's plan anymore.

He faced her again. Had he sensed her staring?

Patting her arm, he offered, "It will be all right, I promise. We'll be there soon enough."

Soon enough? Oh, yes, to Victor.

Frank was as kind as he reasonably could be, and he did seem to care for her. Though she wouldn't say he loved her. Not in the same way that...she had once thought Timothy did.

"Frank," she started, fighting a wave of nausea. "What do you hope for our life together?"

He looked up then shut his book somewhat reluctantly. "I hope for a quiet life. One in which we care for each other and get along well enough." He smiled and turned back to his book.

That didn't sound bad. Though it didn't sound thrilling and adventurous either. Is that what she wanted? This quiet life? It did not intrigue her.

"And why do you want to marry me?"

This time he shut his book a bit harder. "Why do I want to marry you? It should be obvious."

Now was a time for honesty. "It's not to me."

"I find you rather amiable. Docile. And not infatuated with material things. You certainly won't hurt my bank account, and you'll be a good housewife." He touched her hand. "There. Is that better?" Then he opened his book again.

For certain, he was being as forthright as possible. She could trust that. But it didn't stir any excitement in her. Yes, he would take care of her and expect her to do her part in turn, but nothing in his profession spoke of love.

"How do you feel about me?" she ventured, startled when he shut his book for the third time and shifted his upper body toward her.

"I don't know where this is coming from. I thought we had settled this kind of thing."

She shook her head slowly. "Not for me."

He sighed. "I'm not the sort of fellow that fawns over women or gives credence to those types of feelings. But I'd like to think I'm prudent and wise with the decisions I make. I didn't come to this desire to marry you quickly. It was the product of much thought and consideration. Especially with your...situation."

She couldn't fault him. He had never given her any other illusions about his feelings. But, somewhere, somehow, she still wanted him to *feel* something. To want to marry her for more than just consideration.

The stagecoach slowed.

Jane glanced out the window and saw buildings around them. They had arrived in Victor.

"I'll mention our walk to the driver." Frank turned to open the door.

Jane grabbed his arm. "I don't think I can marry you." The statement surprised even her. Would God take away even this final opportunity that, in truth, she was grasping at?

"What?" His eyes reflected his surprise even as they darkened a bit.

Despite her desire to blame God, she knew this was her own doing. And, as such, she needed to be party to the undoing. No matter how difficult it might be. "I'm sorry, Frank. I truly am. I just... don't know that this is enough for me."

He settled back against the seat and stared ahead for a moment.

The sounds of men unloading and loading mail filled the silence between them.

"You know," Frank said, his words delivered slowly and carefully. "I'm likely to be your best offer, if not your only offer."

She sucked in a breath.

"What do you expect with your...situation? Not many men, if any, will find that acceptable."

She bit at her lip. What he said was true.

"I thought we wanted the same things, Janie. You agreed to marry me."

"I understand. But I don't believe I will be happy. And that will only lead to regret and difficulties. I can't consign myself to that life when there may be hope...albeit a small hope...for something more." Could she believe that? Could she trust God for something more?

He laughed. "You are indeed ridiculous. Are you completely unaware that, despite your challenges, you are old enough yet that you will be a spinster? Is that what you want? To live life alone?"

She let out her pent-up air, her face heating at his insinuation. "I would rather live alone, than live with regret."

His features softened. "Janie, I—"

Shouts filtered in through the window, distracting both of them from their exchange. What was going on?

Then she caught one word clearly enough: "Fire!"

Timothy pushed his horse harder and prayed the animal would be able to sustain the pace for a bit longer. He had to get to Victor. He had to find her, to tell her.

Why had he fought this so hard? And for so long? It didn't make any sense now. Of course, he loved her. All of her...regardless of what the future may hold.

It could be that whatever God had for him included the inter-twining of their paths. Was that possible? Could God be so good as to grant him this gentle mercy in opening the way for him to be with her?

How could he have thought he could let her go? His heart hammered in his chest at the prospect that he might be too late. He just couldn't lose her. Not now. Not after realizing...

He oscillated between praying and searching the area. He ached for direction from the Almighty...assurance...something. But as he scanned, everything was as it should be—brown, sparsely dotted with vegetation. And open...no stagecoach in sight. No surprise there. Jane and Frank had likely reached Victor unless something unfortunate had happened. Like an accident. Or bandits.

Prayers went up once more, asking God to keep Jane safe. Even if that meant Timothy had lost his chance. He couldn't bear the thought of something horrible befalling her.

He urged the horse up what he hoped was the last rise. And paused to look toward Victor.

Something wasn't right. Timothy halted the horse completely.

The animal heaved and snorted. As if the mare were both eager to continue and worn from the journey.

There, on the horizon, stood the small town of Victor. But there was a haze of sorts. And...smoke!

A fire had engulfed a portion of the town. Timothy's heart skipped a beat. Then, as he gathered his wits, he pressed the horse onward. His mission was now all more imperative. What if Jane needed help? If she were in danger?

Driving the horse even harder now, he was certain he strained the animal to its very limitations. But the buildings grew closer. It satisfied his heart only somewhat. This urgency within made him wish he could sprout wings and fly.

Soon enough, he entered the edge of Victor. It buzzed with activity. People rushing about with water pails and blankets. Others running to get away from the flames. Thankfully, it seemed as if the fire were contained to one building. He dismounted in a second and scanned the area.

A man rushed by. And though Timothy hated to be so single minded, he had to make sure Jane was all right.

"Where's the telegraph office?" he called to the man.

The man paused briefly, his features read his shock. "The telegraph office? Can't you see the town is burning?" He shoved his bucket at Timothy. "If you have any conscience, you'll fill this with water and help us!" Then he rushed off.

Timothy looked at the bucket, his lungs burning from the drastic difference in the air. There was so much smoke. Saving the town was important. Both for the people and for Jane, if she were even still here. If she were, he prayed she had been taken to safety. For once, he prayed she had already moved on from Victor. He could hope.

Turning toward a nearby watering trough, he dunked the bucket and then ran in the direction of the thick black cloud.

Again and again he hauled water. His eyes stung and his muscles protested, but he had to keep at it. A couple of lines had formed in which women and men passed water back and forth to douse flames. But it wasn't helping. The fire had spread, and it now engulfed at least three buildings.

Timothy's body ached for fresh air, but he had to press that to the side and force himself to keep going. These people needed him.

Then he spotted her—there, a cascade of dark hair whipping about as she escorted a child from one of the buildings in the path of the fire. Would that structure, too, be in flames soon?

His heart tore at him to see her to safety even as she helped the small child. That was his Jane, ever concerned about others. Of course, she would be aiding the effort. Had they set up a safe place for the women and children? Maybe it would be best to see them to the opposite side of the main stretch.

Moving to her, everything in him wanted to wrap her in his arms and carry her away from this place, this danger. As he neared her, he gripped her arm and yelled, "This way!"

She turned, surprise registering in her body. But as she looked at him, he saw that it was not, in fact, Jane. And his heart raced anew. Where could she be?

Still, he took the woman's arm. As they started moving, the child coughed. A lot. He was hacking and struggling. The woman bent down to speak to him.

Timothy wasted no time lifting the child and leading the woman down the main stretch to where several other children were being gathered.

He set the child down and the woman nodded her thanks before focusing on the child, who now breathed a little easier.

Timothy wanted to stay and make sure the child was indeed well, but he might only be in the way. And he was desperately needed to continue his efforts against the fire.

As he turned, he spotted the stagecoach settled far enough away to be safe.

He whispered a prayer of thanks.

Hopefully, Jane remained within. Though he couldn't help but ensure that this was the case. So, he ran to the door and pulled it open.

And found Frank inside, alone.

"Where's Jane?" Timothy shouted.

"How am I supposed to know?" Frank fairly growled back. "She rushed off into the fire. Crazy woman."

"What?" Timothy's stomach lurched. Where was she?

"All I know is that I need to get out of here," Frank muttered. "Where is the driver?"

"Probably helping contain the fire." Timothy made no effort to contain the harshness in his tone.

"This is madness!" Frank skittered across the bench. "What am I supposed to do?"

"Get out and help."

Frank looked at him as if Timothy's suggestion was absurd.

It didn't matter. He didn't have time for the coward. He had to find Jane.

CHAPTER 19

Found

Jane's airway was scorched. Heat surrounded her, and her body was warmed by her constant effort. Sweat drenched her dress and she had no doubt dirt and smoke marred her appearance. But she had to help. The town was in a dire situation. And everything seemed to come into focus. This was not God's doing any more than the consequences of her sins were. Or the reality of a fallen world.

Someone beside her fell to his knees, coughing.

She rushed to him and tore at his shirt sleeve.

He resisted, but she was more determined and got the sleeve off.

Then she urged him to cover his nose and mouth with it.

He again fought, but he was clearly weakened by having inhaled too much smoke.

She pointed to the opposite side of the street. "Go!"

He nodded, somewhat reluctantly, before moving in that direction.

Jane understood. This was intense. And they needed every hand available. But not at the cost of lives.

The man had left a blanket on the ground. That's why he had

been that way—he had been closer to the flames, flapping against them with the wet blanket.

She gripped the cloth, which was rather heavy.

Taking a minute to tear off her own sleeve, she wrapped it around her own nose and mouth. She was afraid of getting so close, but this wasn't the time for that. *God, help me endure!* Swallowing her trepidation, she rushed for the building. Throwing the blanket against it again and again.

How long she worked was unclear. Her vision was limited by darkness broken up by bits of bright flame. Where was she? Which way was farther in and which way was out? The confusion that took hold of her was inescapable.

And she knew...she was in a bad situation. She believed the way out was to the right and behind her, but the more she moved that way, the hotter it became, if that were possible.

Her body wracked with coughs, and she pressed the sleeve to her nose and mouth. There was something she should do...but she couldn't remember in her desperation for air.

She began to realize she was going to pass out. What would happen then?

Strong arms gripped her as the world around her faded.

Timothy had her. Most assuredly. But would she be all right? He lifted her into his arms, wanting to hold her to himself. Could that keep her from falling deeper into this darkness?

He prayed it would.

Rushing against the billows of smoke, he pressed on in the direction he knew to be safety. Then, just as suddenly as the smoke had enveloped him, he was free of it.

Jane had been coughing, but she was silent now. And still. Too still.

As he reached the planked sidewalk near the stagecoach, he called for the doctor and laid her down. But he did not release her fully, instead he propped her against his chest.

She was disheveled and smeared with black from head to foot.

He put a hand to the side of her face. "Jane!"

No response.

"Jane, come back!" He couldn't lose her. Not now. Not like this.

God, no...she can't be gone. Pleading with the Lord to spare her, he fought against his own fatigue.

"Please," he cried out. "Help me!"

A woman fell to her knees next to Jane. She had a cool cloth and blotted Jane's face. "Is she breathing?"

Timothy looked to Jane's features, watching for the telltale rise and fall of her chest. Was she? His heart would never be whole again if she wasn't.

The woman put a hand to his arm. "She is. See there?"

Indeed, he spotted a gentle movement in her neck that transferred down into her chest.

Thank You, Lord. Thank You!

He held her to himself and continued to praise God for His goodness.

She shifted against him. Was she coming around?

Pulling back slightly, he delved into her eyes, open just slightly.

As her gaze settled on him, her lips turned up. Only just.

She reached up to touch him but struggled with the movement.

He took her hand and held it to his chest. "Don't worry. You're safe now." A thickness in his throat that had nothing to do with the fire made his words somewhat choked.

"You came." Her words were not much more than a whisper.

But he heard them. "Yes. I did. For you." He rubbed a hand along her features, drinking in the sight of her whole and well as if he were in a desert, and she the life-giving water.

"I..."

"Don't try to talk." His words were almost hoarse, rough, and edged for certain.

She squeezed his hand. "Stay with me."

With all his heart, he said, "Always."

Jane smiled as sunlight warmed her face. Even with her eyes closed, she knew it was so. What would the day bring? Memories of the fire caused her to cringe. Then she remembered Timothy...his arms and his words. Could God be so good?

She opened her eyes. As she looked at the somewhat unfamiliar walls, she remembered that she was in the clinic's recovery room in Cripple Creek. Somehow Timothy had gotten her here after the fire was put out.

"You awake?" Timothy's voice gave her pause. Had he been watching her sleep?

She turned toward the sound. And smiled. "How long have you been here?"

His gaze snagged hers. "I...just couldn't make myself leave you."

"Have you been here all night?" For certain the shock was evident in her voice if he could discern as much from her hoarse statement.

He nodded as he pulled back in a stretch. Then he leaned forward on his elbows onto the edge of the bed. His hand found hers and he intertwined their fingers. "How are you feeling?"

"Sore." Was there any reason to not be honest? "But thankful." Her eyes stung with unshed tears. She was so very grateful for Timothy—for rescuing her, and for his change of heart.

He looked concerned then. "How sore?"

She chuckled. "It is nothing. I'll be fine tomorrow, I am quite certain."

"Good," he said as the creases in his features eased. Then he lifted her hand and kissed her fingers. "I...have a confession."

"Oh?" Was this good news? Or something difficult to say?

"Yeah." He rubbed a thumb over hers. "I am sorry I wasn't honest before."

Now her brow furrowed. "What about?" She managed to push the words out, though everything in her tensed.

He rose a bit to lean over her and press a kiss to her lips. It was slow and far too brief. Then he set his other hand to her face, smoothing over the skin there. "I love you, Jane. So very much."

Her heart filled. She wished she could raise herself up and prolong the contact. But as it was, her body protested any movement.

But she couldn't stop the emotion that welled in her eyes. "Truly?"

"Yes," he said, his mouth widening into a smile. "I'm just so sorry I fought it for so long."

She bit at her lip as tears released from her eyes. "Never mind that. You're here now. That's what matters."

He nodded. "There's more."

She widened her eyes. What could he want?

"I want you to marry me, Jane. I can't promise anything grand, or maybe even stable. But I will love you and take care of you with everything in me."

She shifted to sit, but again her body fought her, and she grimaced.

Timothy slid onto the edge of the bed and lifted her so she was in his arms. "Say you will marry me. Please."

It took several minutes for her to still her shaking lips enough to answer. "You're sure. We'll never have a—"

"We'll have each other. And trust God to fill in all the other pieces. Who knows? He may have a family in mind for us. One of heart rather than blood."

A tear trailed down her face.

"Say you will, Jane."

"Yes. Forever yes."

Then he claimed her lips again. This time with more purpose and passion.

As they parted, she asked, "Will we stay in Cripple Creek?"

"If it's all right with you, God has opened another opportunity.

The church in Victor is in need of a preacher. And I think God has led me to it."

A burst of pride snaked through her. "Oh, Timothy, that's wonderful!"

"It'll be different. And it won't be like Cripple Creek, but—"

She pressed a finger to his lips. "It'll be an adventure."

He nodded, pressing his forehead to hers.

"And there's no one I'd rather go with than you."

As he kissed her yet again, there was a new sense that flowed over her.

She belonged with him. And he with her.

And her heart was full.

Epilogue

Timothy watched as Wyatt straightened his bowtie. He could never get the confounded things right.

Wyatt leaned back. "There."

"Thanks, Doc." Timothy winked.

Wyatt clapped him on the back. "You nervous?"

"Not in the way I thought I might be. This feels so right, you know?"

"I do know." Wyatt smirked. "I felt the same way about Katie."

Timothy nodded. He was tempted toward emotions long buried at the mention of Katie, but they had no sting, no power to them. There was only forgiveness and restoration there.

"I think it's time." Wyatt opened the door for him.

They walked together into the church and to the front. The townsfolk were gathered in the pews. Many smiling. All was as it should be.

Timothy spotted Lemuel and his father about halfway back. A pang of guilt threatened as Timothy thought, with regret, how he had misjudged the man.

Mr. Langley had searched for comfort in the bottom of every bottle he could find, but he had never raised a hand against his son.

And, with Wyatt and Reverend Dawson's help, he seemed to be on the road to a better life without the stuff. All the best for him and his son.

Lemuel's nighttime fits were being treated by Wyatt, and several ladies and men from the church had come together to remake the run down home a more suitable place for them both.

The back doors to the church opened and Katie walked in. A slight swell to her abdomen spoke to the news she and Wyatt had just made known to their friends and family—another Sullivan was on the way.

Timothy was truly happy for them and trusted God for what his future family would look like. Perhaps there were surprises in store for them. God knew best, he was quite certain.

Jane rounded the corner, Tom Matthews escorting her. She beamed at Timothy, and he thought his heart would beat out of his chest. She was here and she was his.

He prayed as he watched her come down the aisle that he would be the man she needed, the man that God had designed him to be. And that they might live out God's plan for them faithfully.

For, indeed, there was no one more suited for him, for the adventure ahead. And, as long as they had faith in God and in each other, they would have everything.

Keep reading for a preview of the next book in the Cripple Creek Series!

Thank you, dear reader, for for reading along with me! If you enjoyed this story, I would sincerely appreciate if you would submit a review. It would mean so much to me!

To read more about these characters, follow along with the Cripple Creek Series. Find it at:

https://saraturnquist.com/cripple-creek-series/

Author's Note

I have really enjoyed returning to Cripple Creek, Colorado of the fictional continuation of this story. It always seemed to me that I needed to tell Timothy's story after the first book was finished...the story of a jilted man who found it difficult to love again. Along with a heroine that would be broken in a different way.

The historical context here would involve the fire in Victor, Colorado (near Cripple Creek). There was a fire in August 1899 (which I played with the time a little here). It lasted five hours and absolutely destroyed the town's business district.

Though the fire is not central to the story, but key in the climax of the character journeys, it was interesting to me how little information is readily available about the fire.

Betsy Callaway had never been so humiliated in her entire life. She was quite certain this was so. What could she do but duck and run? So, she held her breath, kept her head down, and bolted for the nearest exit. Had he seen her?

She was mortified. As much as anyone could be. After all, she was Betsy Callaway, the darling of Cripple Creek. And now, nothing more than a governess. How far she had fallen. From having every hope in the world for a fine match, to...hired help. It was too much.

As she rushed for the door that would bring her some form of escape, she heard a voice call out. "Miss Callaway?"

She could just die.

But she turned toward the telegrapher.

"You left your ticket."

She glanced around then slinked toward the counter. There were so many eyes on her. Too many. Didn't these people have anything better to do? Dare she glance in his direction and see if he had noticed?

If he had, he gave no indication. Nick Hammond was talking adamantly with another man. She prayed his attention on the conversation would hold.

As the son of Cripple Creek's banker, a man who had grown up with much privilege, he could not know how she struggled.

"Miss Callaway," the telegrapher called out even louder. He seemed irritated. Well, so was she.

She hurried the remaining distance to the window and grabbed for her ticket.

The telegrapher all but rolled his eyes. Who cared if he was bothered? She certainly didn't. All she cared about was not being spotted by…

She spun and smacked into a wall. Or what she hoped was a wall. But as she glanced up, she renewed her prayers for death to come swiftly. For the young Mr. Hammond stood, broad and tall…and he was looking down at her.

Maybe he wouldn't recognize her. *If only.*

"Betsy?" There was a twinge of amusement in his voice.

"Why, I didn't see you there, Nick." She stepped back and pulled out her fan, attempting to wave away the red that likely rose in her face. Maybe he would think it due to the heat.

"That much is clear." He grinned.

She could just smack that smug smile off his face. Longed to. But that wouldn't relieve her from this predicament.

"What brings you to Colorado Springs?" His eyes danced, proving that his carefree attitude from childhood had not changed. As schoolmates, she had continually been frustrated by his tendency to make everything and anything a farce for his own amusement.

Unfortunately, some of their classmates had enjoyed his wit. The lack of a larger group to laugh with him was her only saving grace.

"I am…" She fanned herself faster, her gaze darting about. But no one paid them any mind. Then she returned her focus to him. "It's not really any of your concern." Her words took a sharper turn than she'd meant.

Nick jerked back as if her tone bit at him.

Just as well. It wasn't as if she wanted to renew their childhood acquaintance. She had not seen him in Cripple Creek for near on five years. So, there was little point in ingratiating herself to him now.

"I only wondered," he muttered.

"What was that?" She firmed her expression, determined to not let anything give.

"I only wanted to express how good it is to see you." His smile—a grin that had always been a little too charming—spread across his features. "You are looking good…I mean, well. You are looking well."

She frowned and stuck her nose in the air. "I did not invite you to look."

His grin fell. Quickly. "Same old Betsy." He sidestepped and started for the door.

"And what is that supposed to mean?" She should let him go. And be thankful he did so without a further word. But she couldn't help herself. Why give him the satisfaction?

He spun, appearing just as surprised at her words as she. He scanned the small office. Was he looking for reinforcements? More friends to join him in laughing at her? At length, he shrugged. "You always did have a way with words."

Her fan halted and her look became a glare. There was no way she would let him know how his words pinched at her. It wasn't as if he looked any better off. In fact, his dusty trousers and wrinkled plaid shirt told a different story than the suits his father wore. Perhaps he, too, had fallen from grace.

Her lips parted, but she stopped her comment before it was uttered. They were not the same. They had nothing in common except some rather unfortunate schoolyard memories. That was all.

"If you'll excuse me, I have a stage to catch." With that, she grabbed for her skirts, whirled away from him, and stomped outside.

A rush of wind and dust assaulted her senses. She cringed, wishing she was anywhere but here. But she refused to let Nick Hammond tell her what was and what should be. His judgment stung, but she wouldn't have it. Not today. Not with what she faced.

Another woman, perhaps the same age as Betsy, bedraggled and slumped, made her way to the platform, a small girl at her heel. The child's blonde ringlets and pink bows reminded Betsy of herself at that age.

"Mama, when will the stage be here?"

"Soon, dear," came the woman's tired response. Indeed, everything about her looked haggard. Perhaps that just came with mothering. She'd seen many a mother who seemed thusly fatigued.

Not that Betsy's mother ever had a hair out of place. From the look of this woman, she had hastily pulled her hair up. And even now, pieces fell from her pins here and there. The woman had clearly spent more time on the child's appearance. Was this a glimpse at what Betsy would be like in a few months? The two children she had been hired to mind and teach were young. Their mother had described them as being 'full of life.' Betsy was no dunce. She knew that meant 'difficult.' But she hadn't many other options.

She'd become an old maid. Done for, before her time had come.

The small child bounced on the balls of her feet as if she could spot the stage better that way. Her gaze caught on Betsy, and she smiled widely. How innocent. How naïve.

Her mother glanced about as well. Only she appeared to be concerned about something.

"Excuse me, miss." The woman's warm, worn voice called to Betsy.

These two would likely be on the stage with her. Dare she ignore the woman and face an even more uncomfortable ride to Denver?

"Yes?" Betsy tried to put a kindness she didn't feel into her words.

"Do you know...has the stage come?"

"Not yet. But it's due any minute."

The woman nodded and thanked Betsy.

"I'm Diana," the small girl announced.

Who was she talking to? Betsy chanced a glance and found a pair of dark blue eyes staring up at her. Could she just ignore the child? Maybe if she didn't look at her more than necessary...

"What's your name?" The girl was unfazed.

"Leave the nice lady alone," her mother admonished.

Betsy nodded at the young mother, relieved she wouldn't have to play nice. That thought struck her. How was she to manage two 'lively' children if she couldn't even answer this girl's simple question? She fought back the sting of moisture in her eyes. This was not how she had planned her life. It was not what she wanted.

But none of that mattered. It was what she faced just the same.

Movement at the door drew her attention. But it was only Nick Hammond and the other man exiting the establishment.

She jerked away, but not before Nick tipped his hat in her direction with another too-wide grin. Again, would it be terribly rude to smack it from his face?

Then a thought hit her...was he on this stage too? She shut her eyes and decided the Lord could not be so cruel... But He had been—landing her in a situation she loathed and then topped it with this uncomfortable interaction.

But Nick and his companion moved off farther into town.

Maybe God had heard her. Maybe.

But she doubted it. Why would He start now?

Rumbling in the air told that something large approached. Sure enough, the stagecoach rounded the strip of buildings on the edge of town and barreled toward the small group.

Destiny had come for her in a dust-covered and mud-marred coach. A far cry from Cinderella's grand carriage. And this one would not bear her to a prince, but to a family in Denver. She sighed as she looked at Nick's retreating form. At least it would take her far from that ogre.

And that, she was truly grateful for.

To read more, find *Love in Cripple Creek* here:

https://saraturnquist.com/love-in-cripple-creek/

Hope in Cripple Creek (Book 1)

Tragedy strikes Katherine Matthews and the small town of Cripple Creek, Colorado. An epidemic teams her with an old enemy, Wyatt Sullivan, the town's doctor. In the midst of desperation and death, Katherine has decisions to make. But she has no idea to what extent they will affect her daily life and livelihood.

Katherine faces a crisis of faith and hard choices. Will life ever be normal again?

Christmas in Cripple Creek (Book 2)

Katherine and Wyatt have settled into a well-earned, comfortable life together. Until an unexpected attack threatens to bring an end to their happily-ever-after. And on the cusp of the town's yuletide merriment.

As they come to grips with their new circumstances, they begin to realize the difficulty is far from over. And new challenges arise.

What will become of their family? Of their Christmas?

Love in Cripple Creek (Book 4)

A woman burned by love. A man who has lost his way.

Betsy Callaway hasn't been the most upstanding person in Cripple Creek...and she has now passed the acceptable age for marriage. But something about her calls to Nikolai "Nick" Hammond's heart and draws him back home.

The antics that ensue between the pair and the obstacles they face--including their own stubbornness and becoming entangled in a bank robbery-- threaten to keep them on separate paths, but their draw to each other pushes them together.

**Will the prodigal find home welcoming?
Can Betsy hope for real redemption?**

And the prequels...

Lauren Crawford is nothing she should be. Put off by the War between the States and her own experience on her father's plantation, she longs for something more. Under the control of her parents, there is not much room for anything but submission. Still, she dares to defy them...

The war changed Tom Matthews. And he has plans of going beyond his father's humble farm. He will do whatever it takes to make those dreams come true. Until he finds himself drawn to a southern belle he would rather despise. He is soon caught up in a situation not of his own making.

How much is too much for the one he loves?
Dare he sacrifice his dream?

In the rugged terrains of Cripple Creek, David Matthews' world has always been overshadowed by his father. Each sunrise over Stoneybrook Ranch reminds him of the path laid out before him—a life scripted by expectations he isn't sure he can live up to.

Mary Foster has held a silent affection for David since their youth. And while her mother suffers the ravages of a disease they fight to contain, Mary's heart patiently beats in the hope that when David finds his place in the world, there might be room in it for her.

Will their paths diverge in the vast expanse of the frontier?
Or perhaps love can guide them to find in each other the very thing
they are lacking in themselves—home.

Acknowledgments

It's time to thank everyone who played a part in the creation of this book.

First off, Cindy Smith and Kelly Hollman...wow. Without your input and plotting help, this story just wouldn't have made it. Thank you!

For my Word Weavers group, I appreciate your patience and feedback each month. Your responses on this story were no exception.

For my Novel Academy Huddle, thank you for your tireless support and encouragement when the writing journey gets difficult.

VerBull photography, I love the headshot. You always get my "good side."

Julie Sherwood, you help my stories shine when you add your efforts via editing. These works wouldn't be as solid and polished without you!

Becky Brabham, you give my characters life through your art and narration. Amazes me every time.

Cora Graphics, thanks for all the work you do on the covers. This one was a fun collaboration!

To my family, thank you for the love and support you give so tirelessly.

And to my readers, thank you for giving me a reason to return to the keyboard. Every. Time.

Sara is a coffee lovin', word slinging, Historical Romance author whose super power is converting caffeine into novels. She loves those odd little tidbits of history that are stranger than fiction. That's what inspires her. Well, that and a good love story.

But of all the love stories she knows, hers is her favorite. She lives happily with her own Prince Charming and their gaggle of minions. Three to be exact. They sure know how to distract a writer! But, alas, the stories must be written, even if it must happen in the wee hours of the morning.

Sara is an avid reader and enjoys reading and writing clean Historical Romance when she's not traveling.

Please follow along with her journey through her newsletter at: http://saraturnquist.com/list

Happy Reading!

facebook.com/AuthorSaraRTurnquist

instagram.com/sararturnquist

x.com/sararturnquist

youtube.com/@SaraRTurnquist

pinterest.com/sararturnquist

Also by Sara R. Turnquist

CONVENIENT RISK SERIES

A Convenient Risk

An Inconvenient Christmas

A Less Convenient Path

A Convenient Escape

An Inconvenient Acquaintance

These Golden Years

A Less Convenient Arrangement

Ranch Hands Collection (ebook only)

LADY OF BOHEMIA SERIES

The Lady Bornekova

The Lady and the Hussites

The Lady and Her Champion

The Lady and Her Secret

RAILWAY ROMANCE SERIES

Laura, The Tycoon's Daughter

ACROSS THE YEARS SERIES

Among the Pages

Between the Lines

STANDALONE NOVELS

www.ingramcontent.com/pod-product-compliance
Lightning Source LLC
Chambersburg PA
CBHW061817190726
48289CB00007B/2232